MW00903114

MORTIMER: rat race to SPACE

MORTIMER: rat race to SPACE

JOAN MARIE GALAT

DCB

Copyright © 2022 Joan Marie Galat
This edition copyright © 2022 DCB, an imprint of Cormorant Books Inc.
This is a first edition.

No part of this publication may be reproduced, stored in a retrieval system
or transmitted, in any form or by any means, without the prior written consent
of the publisher or a licence from The Canadian Copyright Licensing Agency
(Access Copyright). For an Access Copyright licence,
visit www.accesscopyright.ca or call toll free 1.800.893.5777.

We acknowledge financial support for our publishing activities: the Government of
Canada through the Canada Book Fund and The Canada Council for the Arts;
the Government of Ontario, through the Ontario Arts Council, Ontario Creates,
and the Ontario Book Publishing Tax Credit. We acknowledge additional funding
provided by the Government of Ontario and the Ontario Arts Council
to address the adverse effects of the novel coronavirus pandemic.

LIBRARY AND ARCHIVES CANADA CATALOGUING IN PUBLICATION

Title: Mortimer : rat race to space / Joan Marie Galat.
Names: Galat, Joan Marie, 1963– author.
Identifiers: Canadiana (print) 20220218196 | Canadiana (ebook) 2022021820X |
ISBN 9781770866539 (softcover) | ISBN 9781770866546 (HTML)
Classification: LCC PS8613.A459192 M67 2022 | DDC JC813/.6—dc23

United States Library of Congress Control Number: 2022935773

Cover art: Julie McLaughlin
Interior text design: Tannice Goddard, tannicegdesigns.ca

Manufactured by Houghton Boston in Saskatoon,
Saskatchewan, Canada in August, 2022.

Printed using paper from a responsible and sustainable resource,
including a mix of virgin fibres and recycled materials.

Printed and bound in Canada.

DCB Young Readers
AN IMPRINT OF CORMORANT BOOKS INC.
260 SPADINA AVENUE, SUITE 502, TORONTO, ON, M5T 2E4
www.dcbyoungreaders.com
www.cormorantbooks.com

For Brae Amelia.
May your dreams take you to heights
even greater than you imagine.

CHAPTER ONE

WATCHING ASCANS

MY LIFE IS pretty sweet, at least for my kind. As long as I'm careful, I can come and go as I please. Nobody is going to cut me open to peer at my insides. I have a roomy pad, regular food deliveries, and a journal to write in. The only experiments I take part in are tests to measure intelligence, like how fast I can get through a maze. Superfast, by the way.

All this leaves plenty of time for my hobby — observing AsCans. That's short for astronaut candidates — not what you might be thinking. I watch AsCans in Houston, at the Johnson Space Center. It's where astronauts train to go up in space. With more than two hundred buildings near the edge of Clear Lake, it sprawls like a city. There's always something going on, even if you're a *Rattus norvegicus*. If you don't know your Latin, that's the scientific name for lab rat, but most just call me Mortimer.

One morning, I put my eye to the peephole I gnawed through the drywall and crane my neck to see the AsCans staring at a picture of a spacecraft. A flutter trills through me. I love that humans want to go to Mars. It may take them years to figure out how to keep people alive on such a distant planet, but it's going to happen. We're going to Mars one day. I lean forward to hear the speaker. He jabs a remote control and bellows like a foghorn. "There are a lot of problems to solve before you AsCans get to the Red Planet. For starters, we need to find a way to ship two years of food without using too much fuel. Then we have to land it safely on the surface."

The next picture shows condiments. Dozens of them! Jars of everything, from garlic juice to screaming hot sauce, litter a table. "Taste buds don't work well in space." Foghorn licks his plump lips. "Lucky for you, food scientists work on ways to make meals taste better up there."

I shake my head. Imagine — scientists who specialize

in food! The next shot shows unmentionable items of clothing. Are there underwear scientists too?

Foghorn wags the remote. "Don't expect to wash your underthings in space. There's not enough water. You'll wear all your clothes 'til they reek, then you'll throw them out."

The AsCans begin to whisper. Are they upset about the waste? Last week's speaker said it costs $10,000 for every pound of supplies they ship into space. I lean an ear to the hole.

"Rats! This really sucks."

"The same ratty underwear for a week, yuck!"

"This is not acceptable! Even in space, life's a rat race."

Why do they have to compare the bad things to rats? Humans can be nasty. I force out a breath and peer up at the next picture. It's labeled "Sleep Station." Foghorn blathers about how every astronaut will have a sleeping bag and a special spot to sleep. Each one will also have a net to hold earplugs, eye masks, headphones — all the things they might want nearby.

This time I forget to muffle my snort. "What do they need all that stuff for if they're asleep?"

"No idea!"

I spin around. Celeste's narrow face is inches from

4 · JOAN MARIE GALAT

me. Her pellet breath fills my lungs. Celeste is my neighbor in the lab. Sometimes I read her bits from my journal, and sometimes, when the scientists spot a pen in my wood chips and take it back, she lets me borrow one from her collection.

Celeste puts her eye to the peephole. "They do seem to go overboard with the details," she says.

"Rats are much more suited for colonizing Mars, don't you think?"

"I'm sure we are," says Celeste. Drywall dust trickles down her face, and she sticks her pink tongue out to taste it. "But I'm okay sticking to Earth. Everything I need is here."

"Doesn't it bug you that no one notices anything good about us? We're intelligent and inquisitive. We adapt to new environments — no problem. Yet across the planet, humans ignore rats."

Celeste nods, but her ears prick. I hear it too — pawsteps. It's probably Romano, scavenging for stuff humans threw away.

I talk faster, and my tongue trips over itself. "Nobody even knows about our most famous rats! Is there a statue of the first one to step ashore from the ships that brought us here from Europe in 1775? What about rats in literature? Are there any cities named after Templeton in *Charlotte's Web*? Any gardens named for Ratty in *The Wind in the Willows*?"

Our noses detect his musky odor at the same time. Romano is close.

My hind foot taps. "Do you know people even dress up like their heroes? I saw it on Halloween. Why isn't anyone dressing up like Remy from *Ratatouille*?"

Celeste opens her mouth to answer just as Romano arrives. He's what humans in the lab call an odd-eye — one is red, like a dark ruby, the other black. I step closer to Celeste so I can only see the black one. Romano is holding a cotton work glove.

"Are you looking for the other hand?" I waggle my ears. Romano is crazy about shredding cloth and building nests. He's got hideouts everywhere.

"I'm looking for you two!" Romano flicks his tail at our noses. "Iceberg Hands left early for lunch."

"She never goes early!" I jump back and jam a pawful of drywall dust into the peephole.

Celeste is already picking her way back through the wall. "Hurry, or she'll know we can get out," she calls back, then turns to Romano. "Thanks for finding us," she says. "You're a real pal."

"Yeah, thanks." I pause to rub dust from my eyes. "Thanks a lot."

"I'll see you back there," says Romano. Rolling the glove into a ball, he jams it behind a board, then trots back the way he came.

"Wait!" I call. "What happened?"

"Her phone rang," says Romano. "Then she looked at her calendar and tore out of the lab."

Romano disappears, and I trot to catch up to Celeste. "The AsCans were driving me crazy, anyway. They worry about ketchup and clothes instead of focusing on the most important thing — how to stay alive on the thirty-four-million-mile trip to Mars."

Celeste glances around. "When that underwear slide went by, I thought your head was going to pop off your neck!"

"It's the way they talk." Catching up, I nearly step on Celeste's snaky pink tail. "You heard them. Every mean thing they say has 'rat' in it. Dirty rat. Rat fink. Looks like a drowned rat."

Celeste stops at a golf ball–size hole in the lab wall and waits for me.

"Rat on someone. Rug rat. Mall rat."

We peer into the lab. Romano gives us the *no humans* sign — forepaws together.

My limbs go limp with relief. I turn to Celeste. "Pack rat. I smell a rat. Rat race."

We bolt along the row of lab rat cages. Celeste chirps, "Like rats leaving a sinking ship!"

"That's what I thought you were doing." Gorgonzola curls his lip.

I bite mine. *Hello, least favorite neighbor. Glad to see you, too.*

Gorgonzola jumps to his exercise wheel. "Now that you're back, you can watch me ace the maze. Today's fastest speed wins a spot on the International Space Station."

Is he serious? A chance to visit the ISS? I don't answer, but that never stops Gorgonzola, even at a full gallop on a squeaking wheel.

"I'll be orbiting Earth, chowing down on space pellets. You'll be stuck here, spying and scribbling in your book. What a waste of time." Jumping from the wheel, Gorgonzola runs his paw along the mesh like it's a piano keyboard. He knows I hate that sound.

My hind paw begins to tap. I should be the one to go to the ISS! The problem is, Gorgonzola is not lying. He's like lightning in the maze, but speed isn't everything. Halloumi, who can smell trails like a bloodhound, beats him on nose-power alone. The only time Halloumi loses is when his allergies flare. His sniffer is no good when it gets stuffed up.

Turning my back to him, I duck around my water dispenser to face Celeste. "Going to Mars is going to be a lot harder than going to the Moon. Don't you think humans spend too much time planning the perfect sleep station and all that cozy stuff?"

Celeste pauses mid-stretch and tilts her head. "You gotta remember, they don't have our intelligence."

"I have no problem remembering that! But do you think it's possible to raise the image of the rat?"

"MM." Celeste yawns and flops onto her stomach. MM means "Maybe, Mortimer." It's part of our private code. She's using it because she's about to nap and wants me to wrap it up. Trust Celeste to find a nice way to say, "Shut up."

"I just wonder what it would take," I say.

Celeste's eyes are closing.

"MIWTYM."

"What?"

"Maybe it will take you, Mortimer — MIWTYM."

Crossing to the other side of her cage, Celeste curls into a ball. I'm dismissed.

Gorgonzola snorts. Ignoring him, I rock on my paws. The space program could change everything for ratkind. We could go to Mars without fifteen different condiments to flavor our food. We wouldn't need an enormous supply of clothes to hide our private parts. We could get by without special places just to sleep.

Don't get me wrong. Humans still need to be part of the space program. After all, they're good at building things like rockets and satellites. They designed the International Space Station. They even got it zooming around the Earth at 17,150 miles per hour. Less work for me.

I burrow into my wood chips. The crisp scent of shredded aspen usually soothes me. This time, it doesn't stop the question in my mind: What will have to happen to make rats the chief species to colonize Mars?

A clicking sound distracts me. Peering out, I see an AsCan slide a computer mouse across a pad.

That's another thing. It should be called a computer rat.

Rolling to one side, I watch him tap out a tweet.

"Maybe I should use Twitter," I mutter. "It worked for Chris Hadfield. The whole world paid attention when he was in space."

Something in my stomach flips, and I jump up. Why not use scientific evidence to make my point? Living on the space station would be the perfect opportunity. I could run experiments to prove rats are better suited to colonizing the Red Planet and share my results with the world.

Or, as scientists like to say, I would "communicate my findings." They love to complicate things with fancy words. Twitter's not my style, but I could set up a YouTube channel. Maybe call it RatTV. I'll be Mortimer, Rat AsCan Extraordinaire. There's just one problem. How can I beat Gorgonzola in the maze?

CHAPTER TWO

ICEBERG HANDS

I DECIDE TO warm up for the race on my exercise wheel. I'm about to jump on when I spot Gorgonzola twist a paperclip into his door latch. He wiggles the wire until the door pops open, then scuttles to a cabinet and disappears inside. If I squint, I can just make out the label on the door: "Plant and Pollen Samples."

Is anyone noticing this? I scan the other cages, but no one else is watching.

Gorgonzola slips from the cupboard with a pocket-sized manila envelope in his mouth. I duck, force myself to count to five, then inch upward. He is slinking toward Halloumi's cage. A low buzz comes from a pile of wood chips. Halloumi is snoring.

Wheels rattle down the hallway. Gorgonzola hears it too. He sprints to Halloumi's cage and dumps the contents of the envelope through the top. Dark green flakes drift down as Gorgonzola turns and disappears into the cabinetry. The envelope flutters to the floor.

Halloumi scrambles from his nest and blinks a few times before trotting across the chips to inspect the flakes. I want to warn him Gorgonzola is up to something, but I'm no rat fink. Should I just whisper, "Be careful"?

Before I can decide, Halloumi pushes his nose into the flake pile. He jumps back, and his head judders like a clucking chicken. "*Ratchoo, ratchoo, ratchoo!*" It sounds like a row of war cannons and blows the envelope to the floor, label up. I read *Helenium autumnale.* That's common sneezeweed!

Halloumi tries to shove an armload of flakes out the side of the cage, but handling them makes it worse. He sounds like a honking Canada goose. My entire body begins to quiver as I realize what Gorgonzola's stunt means. Halloumi will be too stuffed up to smell his way through the maze. Gorgonzola is cheating to get to space!

Halloumi buries the rest of the flakes by turning his nose away and pushing with his hind paws. He finishes just as Iceberg Hands arrives, pushing a whiteboard into the lab. Its wheels clatter as she butts it up to the maze. Grabbing a black marker, she scrawls the names of the lab rats being tested: Celeste, Romano, Feta, Munster, Wigmore, Tillamook, Halloumi, Mortimer, and Gorgonzola. All the rats besides Celeste and me were born in this lab and are named after a type of cheese. Celeste came from a different lab, and I was brought in as a rescue rat — a humiliated, unwanted, discarded pet. Why was I discarded? For chewing things and swimming in the toilet. You know, what rats do.

I watch Iceberg Hands start the health checks and hope Halloumi won't have another sneezing fit. Gorgonzola cannot get away with this!

After inspecting each rat, Iceberg Hands trades her stethoscope for a stopwatch, then readies the start gate. For all their smarts, humans don't know we smell the path of the rat who has gone before, or that the tiny notches we make show the shortest route to the food. No matter how we feel about one another, that's the rule. Make it easier for the next rat. Always stick together.

Gorgonzola's stunt makes me want to beat him more than ever. He's never going to help prove rats are meant for Mars. I've been dreaming of stopping the way people talk about us ever since Chester, the kid from my former home, said, "Take that useless rat away."

Keeping one eye on the second hand of the clock, I watch Celeste, Romano, and Feta work the maze. Not bad times, but by being first they don't have the same advantage as the later rats who follow the smells and notches.

"I don't want to go to space anyway," Celeste whispers to me. "Neither do Romano and Feta. It would mean starting fresh hoards, and there's barely any gravity on the ISS. All our stuff would float away."

Nodding, I watch Munster. His time is decent, but Wigmore isn't so lucky. He gets a serious itch. Stopping to scratch turns him around. By the time Wigmore realizes he's going backwards, he's got no hope of a good time. I still have a chance.

"Check out Tillamook," I whisper to Celeste. "She's going to be serious competition."

Nose to the floor, Tillamook zips through the maze. Notching doesn't slow her down a bit. When Iceberg Hands writes 124 seconds on the board, my hind leg starts to tap. Feta and Romano cheer. Munster presses his lips together.

Iceberg Hands reaches for Halloumi. I can tell he's still stuffy from the way he squeaks when the stethoscope touches his chest. Iceberg Hands scribbles on her paper, then flips through the pages on her clipboard. Did she hear something in his lungs? She turns back to the top page, lowers her head to give Halloumi one last look over, then awards a checkmark. I hop straight up in the air, but Gorgonzola slaps his tail. Our eyes meet, and he curls one side of his lower lip back. Celeste and I call it GG — the Gorgon grimace.

As we turn to the maze, I feel Celeste's glance. She's wondering why I'm happy Halloumi will compete, but I can't explain. I'd have to fink on Gorgonzola, and that would make me as bad — well, nearly as bad — as him.

Halloumi dashes out of the gate, nose twitching. He usually gains speed at the junctions, but this time, he's hesitating. The stopwatch records a dismal 152 seconds. Gorgonzola jumps in the air, and Halloumi clenches his jaws as Iceberg Hands drops him in his cage.

It's my turn. Iceberg Hands cradles me until she's warm and I'm shivering. Maybe it was her glove Romano found. After recording my weight, she peers at me through scratched lab goggles. If my eyes water, crimson goop oozes from my nose, or any other oddity suggests I might be less than a perfect specimen of rat-kind, she'll take me out of the race. I try to be patient, but it's not my style. I *really* have to try.

Finally, I'm at the starting point. I need to beat 124, and my time has to be so good, Gorgonzola won't be able to top it. My heart pounds as Iceberg Hands lifts the gate. I dart forward, sniffing the trail. Tiny black plops mark the most traveled route, and, nose twitching, I trot deeper into the maze. There's less poop now, and I watch for the clues. A notch means I'm on the right track. A notch with a slash through it means a dead end is ahead. I realize I've messed up when I reach a junction without any notches at all. I'm more off course than anyone else has been in this race! My shoulders slump. I'll never recover the time. Gorgonzola is going to get away with cheating his way to space, and there's nothing I can do about it.

Or is there? Before I can think my idea through, I slash the notches on the through lanes and make fresh notches on the dead ends. Gorgonzola won't have a chance. I know everyone will figure out what I've done, but it's too late. I've done it. Legs pumping, I sprint to the end and watch Iceberg Hands reach for her marker. Thick black strokes announce my time — 142. Eighteen seconds longer than Tillamook. Not quite as bad as I thought. I keep my eyes down as Iceberg Hands lifts me out. I can feel Celeste watching me.

"Mortimer!" she hisses. "What have you done?"

Pretending not to hear, I focus on Iceberg Hands. She listens to Gorgonzola's heart, then plops him into the maze. Everyone follows the second hand as it sweeps around the clock. Gorgonzola has never been so slow. The other rats look at one another. I stare at the clock and try to ignore the exercise wheel spinning inside my stomach. Will Celeste still be my friend? Finally, Gorgonzola reaches the end. Iceberg Hands writes 192 seconds on the board. The only sound is a dripping tap.

Iceberg Hands returns Gorgonzola to his cage and wheels the whiteboard out. I can see the sunlight outside the window growing faint. It's the end of the humans' workday, and she probably won't be back until tomorrow. It seems like a good time to burrow under my chips. I try to keep an equal distance from both Celeste and Gorgonzola. He smashes his water bottle against the mesh. My insides twist, and I'm too scared to peer out. Chatter crisscrosses the lab.

Gorgonzola is hard to miss. "Ought to be taught a lesson." *Smash*. "Wonder what else he's done." *Smash*. "No wonder that kid gave him up." *Smash, smash, smash*.

Romano chimes in, "I should have let him get caught outside the lab."

I dig my nails into a wood chip, glad I can't see that ruby eye staring me down.

"I wonder what else he's done," says Halloumi, and that hurts almost as much as Celeste's disappointed face. Halloumi likes slipping from the lab too, and sometimes we explore together. If he goes out on his own and finds something tasty — last week it was a pile of corn kernels — he always dribbles a few of the treats into my habitat. Now he thinks I dropped sneezeweed into his cage to keep him out of the race. My revenge on Gorgonzola has fully backfired. It will never rain corn again.

"Going to space is important to Mortimer," Celeste says. "It's not right, but he has his reasons."

Celeste is standing up for me! I jump up and scramble to the mesh.

Munster's voice rings out. "I don't care why you think he did it. We have a code."

"I need to go up, Munster, so I can prove rats belong on Mars. Isn't that a good reason? Then we'll all get to go to space." My voice comes out in a high-pitched squeak. I try to sound like a tuba instead. "I can give you a million reasons why —"

"There are a million reasons we don't care what you think." Gorgonzola zings his forepaw across the mesh. "Cheating being the main one. No one is ever going to listen to you."

It's hard to think of an answer to that. I know we should both say we're sorry, but he'll act even more superior if I say it first. Besides, I didn't win. Tillamook is going into space. I drop to my cage floor. Even Chester's disapproval wasn't this bad. I have to get out of the lab.

Fluffing the wood chips to make it look like I'm burrowed in, I reach under my exercise wheel. This is where I hide the treasures humans would take away. I tug out a coarse piece of string the same length as my tail and arrange it to curl out from the pile. Remembering how I found the string in a pool locker gives me an idea. Maybe I can find a video camera, too. I'll give it to Tillamook, and everyone will see I'm trying to make up for what I did. I can't help thinking something sneaky, though. Maybe Tillamook will shoot some video I can use.

I'm lucky to have a cage with a defective latch. Jumping up to hang from a cage bar, I swing my hind legs to pop open my door, then climb out. I close the door behind me and head to the tunnel. Once inside, I choose the passage that leads to the loading zone. The pool is six miles away. I watch a dozen sixteen-wheel trucks come and go, turning my head from the clouds of dust and exhaust that blast toward me. Drivers and passengers hop in and out. I watch work boots, sneakers, and wedged heels go by. You'd notice shoes too, if feet were at your eye level.

Finally, I see my ride. It's a white cube truck with the NASA meatball logo painted on each side. Blue lettering spells out NASA SCUBA.

Leather loafers hop out as I scramble into the narrow space between the cab and cube. Hunkering next to a nub of rubber on the frame, I grab hold. If I'd done that on my first ride a year ago, I wouldn't have bounced into a puddle at the first pothole. Just before the truck takes off, someone jumps up beside me.

Celeste grabs the nub as the truck makes a U-turn. "Where are we going?"

"Uh, the pool." I start to babble. "Of course, the humans don't just call it a pool. It's the largest one in the world, so they gave it a fancy name — the Neutral Buoyancy Lab, or NBL. It's got more water than six Olympic-size pools, enough to fill one hundred and twenty thousand bathtubs."

What I don't tell her is that when I checked it out

last month, Chester showed up on a school tour. I had to hide in a locker room. Seeing him brought back all those whiny taunts: "Dumb rat — not good for anything."

I might have sulked — just a tiny bit — but the locker was a rat's dream. I found the string, my journal, and — best of all — two astronaut pens. When you hold them upside down, the ink still flows. I can lie on my back and still write. Celeste waggled her ears when I gave her one for her pen collection.

I realize she's talking. "You're going to have to make this right, Mortimer. That's all I'm going to say."

"Er, yeah, I know." My head bobs up and down. "Uh, thanks."

She nods. I nod. We're starting to look like bobble-heads when the truck stops in front of the NBL. The click and buzz of cicadas fills our ears as we dart to the pavement and dive through a gap between the doors. It's like stepping into a bleach factory. We toss our tails over our noses, but it's impossible to block the pungent air.

Celeste tries high-speed blinking, but the tears fall anyway. "Humans are terrified of germs, aren't they?"

I find myself nodding again. "If there's one things rats don't have to think about, it's germs making us sick." I wipe my eyes against a foreleg. "Another reason we'll excel on a Mars mission."

We follow the smell of chlorine to the pool.

"Is it really so deep?" Celeste asks.

"I'll show you." I nod for her to follow, and we duck under a cart at the pool's edge. Lying on our bellies, we peer down into the water. The floor is cool, and I feel my fur soak up a plate-sized puddle.

"What's that giant structure down there?" asks Celeste.

Edging forward to look, I lean too far and slide head-first into the pool.

CHAPTER THREE

THE BITE

THE POOL IS warm, like a water bottle left in the sun on a hot day. Sputtering to the surface, I scan the humans. No one is looking. Celeste slides into the water next to me, and we stare. An enormous white tunnel rests on the pool floor, its metal exterior covered in rivets. Black cables snake in neat lines across its surface. It reminds me of three gigantic soup cans, large enough for a golf cart to drive through. My chest begins to quiver. I've seen pictures of this, but not beneath forty feet of water.

I bump Celeste's shoulder. "It's a mock-up of the International Space Station!"

We duck underwater for a better look. When my eyes start to itch, I swim up, shake the water from my face, then plunge back in. I realize the mock-up is as large as the station in space, but this is only part of it. The real one has more modules and enough solar panels to fill a football field. Celeste taps my shoulder and points. Two divers are guiding someone in a spacesuit toward one of the modules. I understand now: AsCans train for working in space by practicing underwater.

Heaving myself out of the pool, I scan for danger, but nobody is close. The fact is, humans are not biologically wired to sneak up on rats. They always announce a sighting with a gasp, scream, or other sign of horror. Instead, I hear digital shutter clicks and a man's gravelly voice.

"Tough to get a good picture with all the glare off the water." Yellow Crocs shuffle around a tripod.

I feel my chest go light. A camera bag rests on the tile, the NBC peacock logo embroidered on its navy canvas. Celeste climbs out of the water, and I point. "I was going to search the lockers for a camera, but look!"

Hunkering low, we creep closer and duck around an orange pylon. A woman with white boat shoes and a "NASA Guide" arm patch stands beside Yellow Crocs.

"The AsCans spend more than one hundred hours in this pool to train for a spacewalk," explains Boat Shoes.

I nudge the pylon closer to the bag, now only three rat lengths away. Celeste's pellet breath heats the back of my neck.

Yellow Crocs brings the camera to one eye. "I notice they wear weights in the water. Is that so they don't bob up?"

"The weights help the astronauts become neutrally buoyant. That means they don't float upward, but because the weights aren't too heavy, they also don't sink. It gives them a feeling close to what it's like to float in space." Boat Shoes speaks in a singsong voice.

Nodding, Yellow Crocs sets the camera in the bag and reaches for a notebook. His silver ballpoint scratches across the page. Celeste looks at the sparkling pen then back at me. We push the pylon together. Two rat lengths. My heart begins to thud.

"It's easier to move heavy objects in water. It's like space, where things take even less effort to move." Using her foot, Boat Shoes pushes the camera away from a puddle. I tug at an ear. Five rat lengths now.

Nodding, Yellow Crocs reaches down to grab the camera. His pen clatters to the floor, and I feel Celeste peer around me. He snaps a dozen more pictures as the astronauts make their way toward the fake ISS. We slide the pylon forward, but it makes a scraping sound. My mouth goes dry, and Celeste freezes, but Boat Shoes is like most people I've observed. More a talker than a listener.

"Two things are different about being in neutral buoyancy." She turns toward the pool. "Astronauts can feel their weight in their suits, and the water's friction slows down their motion. It's like when you sweep your hand through water: you feel the water slowing your hand down. In space, it's different. Astronauts don't feel their weight. They get around with very little effort. When they move their arms, it's like moving through air — there's no water pushing back and slowing their arms down. And when astronauts in space float from place to place, they keep going until something gets in the way, causing resistance."

Nodding, Yellow Crocs reaches for the camera bag. I run a paw through my fur and sigh, then turn to Celeste. "Let's go to the locker room."

"I'll meet you back at the lab," she says, her eyes still on the pen.

Leaving the pylon, I drip down the hallway to the locker room. The first thing I notice is brassy new padlocks hanging on each locker door. Shopping isn't going to be as easy as last time. I'll have to bend a couple of the metal locker ventilation slots apart. Just call me Mortimer, Rat Burglar.

My paws are midair when I hear Boat Shoes. "You can use the washroom in here."

I pop behind a tall white garbage can. Yellow Crocs sets his camera bag on a bench and steps into a stall. My heart starts to thump. The camera is on top, and I can see it's bigger than me, but didn't Boat Shoes just say everything is lighter in space? I dive into the bag.

Turning the camera, I peer at the buttons. *Zoom. Timer. Black and white.* Argh — no video! I'm about to hop out when the stall latch rattles. I freeze. In or out? The door swings open, and I dive to the bottom of the bag, pulling a silky lens cloth over my head. I hear water run, then the rip of a paper towel. Now silence. Is he fussing in the mirror? Is it a good time to hop out? I'm about to peek when Yellow Crocs hoists the bag into the air. Pulling my tail close, I reach for something to hold on to as the bag bangs against Yellow Crocs' pointy hip — *thwack, thwack, thwack.* Trying to reposition myself, I grip something rectangular and force it between the bone and me. Relief! But then something starts to vibrate.

The reporter's hand reaches into the bag. "Sorry," he says. "I'll just turn off my phone."

Dry, calloused fingers sweep through the bag. As I shrink back, something catches one leg. It's a mini camera, smaller than a Rubik's Cube, and it's attached to a head strap. My heart leaps, but there's no time for a closer look. The fingers are tightening around my neck. Instinct kicks in. My incisors sink into a meaty thumb. Rude words are shouted (not by me). The bag crashes down, and Yellow Crocs kicks it across the floor. I tumble inside, but rats know how to handle a fall. When I poke my head out, Boat Shoes demonstrates her ability to scream. Tucking the camera under an armpit, I sprint for the door. The strap flaps behind me.

CHAPTER FOUR

HOORAY FOR FLEAS

GALLOPING ON THREE legs, I plunge through the gap between the outside doors. A huge breath escapes me. The truck is still in the loading zone! Clambering up, I wrap my tail around the nub of rubber. The engine rumbles to life as I turn the camera in my paws to examine my prize. I didn't know they could be made this small! The camera has a chrome button. I push it, my hind leg tapping as I wait to see if it takes a photo. Instead, it beeps several times and the record button lights up. The strap will need some serious trimming, but Tillamook is good with her teeth. I can't wait to give it to her. Maybe everyone will forgive me.

The truck pulls up to the lab, and I duck inside, scanning for humans as I slink along the linoleum tile. Iceberg Hands is writing on a wall calendar, one hand holding a phone to her ear. I dash across the lab and dive into my habitat.

"Right," says Iceberg Hands. "I'll do that now." She spins around. "It's space time, Mortimer."

My ears twitch, and I hear Celeste hiss at me. "Hide the camera."

I shove it beneath the aspen chips, heaping armloads over the strap. "What's she talking about?"

"Tillamook failed the health check!"

"But she was fine before I left!"

"She got fleas from Wigmore. Remember his big itch in the maze? They're both quarantined, and she's disqualified. You're going to space, Mortie!"

A human might belt out a cheer at this point. Rats are subtler. To show my joy, I let my ears drop to each side. I stare at Celeste. Her ears are down too. She's happy for me, and I know I have at least one friend. But my heart is ticking like a too-fast clock. Any minute, Iceberg Hands is going to come around with the stethoscope. I try to breathe the way she does during her lunchtime yoga stretches. In through the nose, out through the mouth. I make a gentle *haaa* sound with each exhale. It feels ridiculous, but my heart stops racing.

Across the lab, Iceberg Hands turns my way. Taking a last look around the cage, I spot my fake tail sticking out of the wood chips. In a leap worthy of any super-hero, I throw myself over the string and shove it out of sight just as her hand reaches for the latch. The smell of aspen wafts upward.

"Aren't you lively today?" she says.

I switch my tail and cock my head to one side. Sometimes that makes her smile, but today Iceberg Hands is all business. I nibble a pellet as she scribbles on her clipboard. She mutters words like "alert," "active," and "good appetite." I take that to mean I have some acting talent.

Picking me up, Iceberg Hands examines my fur for fleas, but I'm clean. Now it's time for the big test. She holds the stethoscope to my chest. *Haaa.* In through the nose, out through the mouth. When she nods and places checkmarks in a series of boxes, I know I've passed. Suddenly my cage is on a cart and I'm rolling to the loading bay. I wave to Celeste and call out "IS, you know!" The others keep their backs turned, but at least she understands — I'm sorry.

Iceberg Hands turns chatty. "Well, Mortimer, you're off to the Kennedy Space Center. It's a long haul — it's in Cape Canaveral, Florida — but all you have to do is sleep and eat. Just like every other day, right?"

I give her a look, but she doesn't notice. How can she forget all the mazes I've run?

"Wait 'til you see the Falcon rocket with its nine engines. Part of me wishes I was going with you to the ISS. The other part, not so much." Iceberg Hands lifts me out, gives my head a scratch, and then does something she's never done before — thank goodness! She kisses the top of my head. "I hope I see you again."

Why does she need to hope? Of course she'll see me again. I'll be back in the lab. I'll also be where she least expects it — on YouTube!

As the truck leaves Houston, I pull out the camera, push the chrome button, and peer through the viewfinder at the cargo around me. A line zigzags across the bottom of every box, no matter which way I turn. My back foot begins to tap. Is the camera broken? Turning it in my paws, I see the square glass on the viewfinder is cracked, but the round lens that focuses the image is fine. I flop against the mesh of my habitat. Videos won't show the jagged line.

I tap the screen and examine the icons that appear along the top of the display. The only symbol I recognize — the one that shows battery life — reads ninety-four percent. I push the chrome button and watch the screen fade to black. Do astronauts bring charging cables to space? I hope so.

I use my teeth to saw through the camera strap, then shorten and knot the ends to make it fit my head. Using the leftover pieces, I weave a ratpack to keep the journal, pen, and camera together. The strap's brown and white camouflage design will make it easier to hide. I wish I'd had something like this when I lived with Chester. He loved to rifle through my cage and take my treasures.

My work complete, I reach for my journal and position the pen using both paws. I would like to report my lettering is exquisite, but writing instruments are designed for fingers and a thumb. I must hold the pen upright like a rocket on a launchpad. Keeping all my letters the same size is tricky. Some sprawl into giants. Others would be easier to read with a magnifying glass. None of that matters to me. A journal is private, not a beauty contest. It's the message that counts.

Dear Journal,

I've overcome the first hurdle — getting a ride to space. Now I can focus on my mission — Proving rats should colonize Mars instead of humans. Even though People are ridiculous on so many levels, they do have their uses. They're trained to supply lab rats with food, water, and shelter. They also know how to construct rockets, space stations, and spacesuits. Still, as I like to say to Celeste, TANBAE — they are not better at everything. Once they see the evidence from my experiments, they'll stop referring to the rat race like it's a bad thing.

    Signing off,

    Rattus norvegicus, also known as Mortimer T. Flightdeck, Future YouTube Sensation

Wrapping my tail around my head, I let the truck's rocking motion lull me to sleep. I dream I'm steering a Mars rover over a rock bed when the vehicle gets hung up on an angular stone. I wake up as the truck bumps to a stop and realize we are at Cape Canaveral. My rocket to the ISS awaits.

The door opens with a squeak, and a wall of heat slams into me. Bright sunlight forces me to squint, and I can just make out neon green laces on dusty work boots. Neon Laces places my cage on a dolly, and it vibrates as he rolls me from the truck. The air is thick with the sweet smell of acacia.

"Welcome to Florida, the Sunshine State," says Neon Laces.

I look up, and his words, the heat, and the smells all fall away. All I can do is stare. I thought the Falcon rocket would be a little taller than a flagpole. Instead, it's as high as an eight-story building and as big around as the largest trampoline. Its shadow is so long, I can't see the end of it. At the very top sits another spacecraft — the Dragon. That's where I'll be riding. I press my forehead to the wire. The Dragon stretches another two stories up, but it's so high it seems tiny way up there, its nose cone pointing toward space. My knees tremble.

Squinting at the rocket's white cylinder, I see the American flag and stand up straighter. It makes me feel stronger — part of something big. Lowering my gaze, I examine the Falcon's nine engines. The liquid oxygen and kerosene propellant that's going to blast us off the planet is super flammable. Is that why Iceberg Hands kissed me goodbye? Is she worried it's *too* flammable?

I grip the cage bars as we bump along the enormous gantry parallel to the rocket. The crisscrossing steel reminds me of monkey bars. Pausing, Neon Laces puts his face to my door. His nose hairs make me want to shudder. At least rat fur is on the outside.

"Hey, fur face!" he says.

Look who's talking. I smooth my whiskers.

"You're getting a sixty-two-million-dollar ride on that baby. I hope you're worth it."

Am I supposed to be impressed with the cost? Rats, of course, do not care about money. That's another way we're superior to humans. Still, I feel a niggle in my chest. Rats can't build stuff like this. I can only hope the humans know what they're doing. Can we really get to Mars?

CHAPTER FIVE

A GIANT LEAP FOR RATKIND

NEON LACES TURNS from the rocket and wheels me into a small brick building. The menacing red letters stenciled on the glass door spell "Quarantine."

"Can't have you getting sick before you become a rocket rat, can we?" Neon Laces plunks my cage on a counter. I sniff. The place is musty.

"It's kind of ratty in here, but that should suit you all right, hey?" Neon Laces scratches an armpit on his way to the door. "Just stay healthy. If the weather's just right in three days, you'll get your fifteen minutes of fame."

My whiskers twitch as I watch him disappear out the door. I am bound to achieve more than fifteen minutes of fame. People are going to notice that rats naturally excel, especially when it comes to adapting to new situations. It's one of the reasons we're suited for the long trip to Mars. AsCans, on the other hand, have to train for at least two years. They also have to stay in the best shape. I decide a few days of physical fitness training will be enough for any ratonaut. Feeling like Mighty Mortie, I gallop on the exercise wheel for as long as it takes to recite the planets five times. Even though Pluto has been demoted to a dwarf planet, I include it. Why should a planet's size and the strength of its gravitational field get it kicked out of the club?

Flopping onto the aspen chips to catch my breath, I reach for my pen.

Dear Journal,

It's time to figure out my Grand Plan.

Step 1: Create experiments that prove humans complicate space travel and rats make better astronauts.

Step 2: Share the evidence on my future RatTV YouTube channel.

Step 3: Await recognition.

Details: Design experiments that compare rats to humans, showing some of the basic differences.

1. RHBTH — rats hear better than humans. (*Rattus norvegicus* will always detect danger before a human has a clue anything is happening. Rats can ensure higher safety standards.)

2. Rats are experts at remaining hidden. (Humans will have a tough time hiding from Martians or other aliens. Hiding will be essential if aliens turn out to be unfriendly — or worse, hungry!)

3. Rats can fall from a height of fifty feet without getting hurt. (Lab rats will have no problem crash-landing on Mars. Even with costly helmets, humans might not survive.)

4. As a species, *Rattus norvegicus* needs less water than humans. (Rats drink less than humans because we're smaller. We don't need to bathe because we groom our fur.)

5. Four paws are better than two hands and two feet. (Rats are more stable with four points of contact on a surface. Humans are too

tall and tippy.)
    That's all for now.
                Signing off,
                Mortimer, Grand Planner

My paws cramp from holding the pen, and I try one of Iceberg Hands' yoga stretches to improve my circulation. I think it's called the downward facing rat.

Repeating the routine every day makes me sleep like a pup, but I always jump up when the technician comes in to do my health check. This guy works faster than Iceberg Hands. Maybe that's why his hands are always damp. I call him Sweaty Palms. If I could mail Celeste a postcard, I'd tell her about Sweaty Palms and ask her something I keep wondering. IESMAM — is everyone still mad at me?

On launch day, my eyes pop open before Sweaty Palms arrives. It's still dark, and the first robin has yet to utter a note. I know NASA will delay takeoff if there is any chance of poor weather. Neon Laces told Sweaty Palms it costs too much to start a launch that the weather might stop. They don't want their million dollars' worth of science experiments to crash into the ocean. I notice not a thought is given to me — the live part of the payload.

Slipping out of my cage, I push the blinds apart. A scattering of stars is trying to hang on to the night, but a sliver of tangerine sky creeps up the slice of horizon between the buildings. I rock from paw to paw. No rain clouds. No thunderstorm. No risk of lightning striking the rocket. As long as a big wind doesn't whip up, it's going to happen. Today.

I duck outside through a floor drain. The air on my fur is warm but not sweltering. Stopping on the tarmac, I inhale. A whiff of diesel tickles my nose, but no vehicles are moving. Did a breeze bring the scent? I lick a paw and hold it up to feel for wind. The robin trills, and its call almost hides the sound of moving air, but there it is. Not like wind. More of a *whish-whoosh*. The spit on my paw cools as the sound gets closer. I look skyward. Outstretched claws are aiming for my shoulders! My eyes lock with the claws' owner — a great horned owl. *What the smell!* I twist to dart away, but it has all the advantages: height, speed, power. Its nails plunge through my fur, and pain splinters through me. I smell iron and feel wet across my back.

Now I'm part of the whish-whoosh. The shadowy ground sinking below makes my chest flutter like a sail. We swoop low over a field, and the swaying knots me even more. I twist and arch, but the claws hold firm. There must be something I can do! I wrench far enough to dig my teeth into a bony toe. The owl jerks its leg, but I clench harder. Clicking its beak in anger, the owl unclamps me. I drop like a spruce cone from a tree.

My scientific side observes how effective gravity is at bringing two objects together. Too bad one of the objects is me and the other is a treeless patch of earth. The shriek I release cannot be stopped. However, as science has shown, such sounds are involuntary reactions to unexpected events, not signs of cowardice.

I land with a graceless thump, inches from a wedge of feldspar. Air rushes from my lungs. I feel like a discarded mitten until finally a proper breath passes through me. Rising to my paws, I stagger down a gopher tunnel, only to come face to face with its occupant. The gopher bares her teeth at me. I press against the dirt wall to give her the right of way, then limp back to the quarantine building. Though spared being a bird's breakfast, I have a new worry. My stomach does not like being airborne. What if, after all my plans, I can't handle spaceflight?

There's no time to dwell on it. I must lick the blood away before Sweaty Palms shows up. It's a good thing I've been doing yoga. Otherwise, I might not have been able to twist far enough around. I swallow the last of the blood as Sweaty Palms arrives.

"You're all set except for one thing." He pulls a weird-looking aquarium from beneath the counter and sets it next to my cage. "Say goodbye to your aspen chips. You're riding in this transporter module. Can't have bits of wood floating around in space."

He cups his slippery hands around me, and before I can even shut my gaping mouth, I'm in the new habitat. It's high-tech — metal, smooth, and shiny. Mesh lines the floor, walls, and ceiling. I squeeze my eyes shut. An eggbeater churns in my stomach. I'm going to space without the camera!

Sweaty Palms loads me onto a cart and pushes me onto the tarmac. I want to bang my head against the food block. My plan depends on having that camera. And what am I going to do without my journal? After Celeste, it's my best friend. I want my lucky astronaut pen, too. Although it doesn't seem to be working.

Circling the module, I see the glass access doors are secured tight. I press the metal walls, but they're reinforced with rivets. People are everywhere. I need privacy and time to work out an escape, but we're already at the base of the gantry.

CHAPTER SIX

CAMERA CRISIS

SWEATY PALMS PUSHES me up to a pair of black work boots with a yellow pinstripe at the ankle. "Rat ahoy," he calls. "Here's your passenger."

"I texted you to wait an hour." Pinstripe puts her nose to my mesh. "We're not ready for live cargo. Even for someone as cute as this. Ever think of paying attention to your phone?"

Cute? I prefer debonair.

Sweaty Palms shrugs. "I'll take him back to Quarantine. Call me when you're ready."

"Just check your texts," says Pinstripe, but she's talking to his back. The detective part of me, also known as RH — Ratlock Holmes — deduces this has happened before.

As the cart bumps along, I throw my shoulders against the food block, but it doesn't budge. I shake the water container. It's not going anywhere. I grab the mesh and try to rattle it loose. It won't even ripple. My shoulders droop. The module is space-travel sturdy.

Back in Quarantine, Sweaty Palms sets the transport module next to my old habitat. I straighten my shoulders. Maybe I can find a loose wire in the mesh. I run my teeth along the walls, starting at the floor. Sweaty Palms tips back a giant, rocket-shaped water bottle, sets it on the counter, then walks over to my old cage. I pause, tooth against wire.

"Might as well clean this out." Sweaty Palms reaches for the pellet dispenser.

His fingers are inches from the camera! Forgetting the wire in my mouth, I spin around, but my tooth catches the wire and pulls the mesh. *Twang!* The sound echoes against the metal walls. It's like being inside a guitar! I hook my tooth and pull again. *Twang!* Will it bring him over? There's no time to check. I angle my jaw again and pull. *Twang, twang, twang!*

A puff of air tickles my whiskers. Sweaty Palms is on the move. I sit on my haunches as he puts his eyes to the transporter module, then flick my tail. Shrugging, he steps back to my old cage. I jump back to the mesh. *Twang, twang, twang!* Sweaty Palms returns, this time unlocking the door. I'm still as he places me in my old cage, but when he turns to inspect the module, I dash to my ratpack. My legs quiver. I still have no way to get it to the new module.

Before I can work it out, Sweaty Palms steps over to bring me back. I crouch in a corner. A trembling rage is growing inside. Everything is Sweaty Palms' fault. I am tired of cooperating. I am tired of his slimy hands. When he reaches in to pick me up, I push against the wall to get as far away from him as possible. It doesn't matter. His arm is long. An aspen chip clings to my leg, and I stick it under my armpit as he lifts me out. I will take something with me!

As Sweaty Palms carries me back to the module, I try to keep my armpit closed, but it's hard to balance. One foreleg slips over the edge of his palm. He opens his hand wider so I can right myself. An opening! I shove the chip in my mouth and leap.

Landing on the counter, I tear across blue tile. Sweaty Palms dashes around the counter. My insides vibrate. Spinning around, I forget to look where I'm going. *Whomp!* My forehead strikes the water bottle.

It lands with a crack, and a tidal wave sloshes over Sweaty Palms.

I scamper back, my chin high. I've always liked a good game of dodge the human. But Sweaty Palms' face is thunderous. Edging closer, he shouts the same rude words as the reporter in the locker room. I must choose — jump to the floor or cross the lake on the counter. I hesitate, and he stretches across the tile. Swampy hands surround me as water gushes to the floor. His eyes flit toward the waterfall, and I jam the aspen chip into the latch as he lowers me into the habitat.

When Sweaty Palms disappears into the bathroom, nervous tingles set a hind paw tapping. I can't hesitate again. Grabbing the mesh, I swing my paws toward the door. *Smack!* It flies open. I leap through the opening and land with a thud. Not my quietest maneuver, but Sweaty Palms doesn't appear. The toilet flushes as I grab the ratpack. Why couldn't rats have thumbs?

I scramble to the transport module and wedge everything under the food block. *Rat-a-tat-tat-tat.* It feels like a woodpecker is in my chest. I hear the squall of a hand dryer as I swing my hind legs, kicking the door to make it bounce shut. The bathroom door squeaks, and Sweaty Palms appears. I hook a tooth in the wire. *Twang!*

"You rat fink!" he exclaims.

Human fink! I reply in my mind, but it doesn't sound as nasty.

Beep! Sweaty Palms glances at his phone screen. "It's time," he says, wheeling me to the gantry. "I wish the astronauts luck with you on board."

Pinstripe raises an eyebrow at his damp shirt. She turns to me. "Take your last breath of fresh air, Mortimer."

CHAPTER SEVEN

PERCHED ON A ROCKET

I INHALE LIKE a yogi as Pinstripe steers the cart into the cargo elevator. Cables rattle as we rumble eight stories up. There's no time to even think a profound thought like "Here we go" or "This is it" or something I might later record in my journal. The elevator shudders to a stop.

Fur prickles on the back of my scalp as I get my first glimpse inside the Dragon. It may be a pressurized capsule, but the Dragon's interior looks like the inside of a well-organized closet. It's lined with aluminum racks, and all the cargo is strapped in place. My nose detects apples, grapes, and green peppers. I can see from the labels that I'm also traveling with crew clothing and computer equipment — even a 3D printer. Pinstripe inserts my module into an opening and gives me a smart salute. I wish I could snap a paw back, but no amount of yoga will give me that option.

"Hang tight," says Pinstripe. "Takeoff will be a while yet." There's nothing to do but wait. I reach for my pen.

Dear Journal,

Here I am perched at the top of a rocket, waiting for liftoff. Here's a list of things I won't miss about Earth.

1. Sweaty human hands.

2. People like Boat Shoes who scream at the sight of you.

3. Bullies like Gorgonzola saying no one will ever listen to me.

4. Ferocious owls with sharp talons and pointy beaks that want to eat you.

5. Gophers that glare at you for using their tunnels.

6. Kids like Chester who like you one minute, but not the next.

Signing off,

Mortimer, Meant for Better Things

I doze a bit, waking with a start when a rumbling makes my ears jut up. Is that the elevator, or is a thunderstorm creeping in? It's hard to pinpoint. The sound seems to surround me. Then I feel it, deep inside my chest. The container labels blur. Everything is shaking.

How can fragile objects survive this? And what about me? I'm a mere sixteen ounces in 4,300 pounds of vibrating cargo. Shouldn't someone be driving this thing? How is it going to travel 250 miles into space and dock without a pilot? Is the Dragon uncrewed because it's not considered safe for human life? Is this why Iceberg Hands said she "hoped" to see me again?

Fully awake now, I understand this is no thunderstorm. It's the ignition of 350,000 gallons of highly explosive rocket fuel under my butt. As the rocket's first-stage engines ignite, I curl into a tight ball, cover my ears, and tuck my head into my chest. (Do not mistake this position for fear! It is simply the official ratonaut safety position for takeoff.)

The rumbling grows, and when the roar reaches its loudest, the shaking multiplies. I squeeze my eyes shut. Fighting gravity with everything it's got, the rocket thunders skyward. My rippling fur feels like it's going to be torn from my skin. As we shoot through the lower atmosphere, the blast of 1.3 million pounds of thrust uncurls my body. My eyes fly open, but I can't focus. Surely my brain is going to rattle out of my head. I make myself count. When I reach 158 — just over two minutes — the shaking lessens. I let out the giant breath I was holding, but my relief is temporary.

According to my eavesdropping, rockets become lighter as they use up fuel. Lighter rockets travel faster. I know that's what's happening because as the Falcon's supersonic speed increases, it feels like my body is being left behind. The sudden thrust feels like a refrigerator full of rocks pushing down on my body. Paws clutch mesh. All my energy is devoted to holding on.

The rocket travels more than ten times the speed of sound. That means that in less than three minutes, this ratonaut travels over three hundred and fifty miles. I'm about to calculate how many seconds it might be before the rocket's last stage separates from the spacecraft when the pressure lifts, and I realize it has already happened. I am in low-Earth orbit. How do I know? That's when the floating begins. My enclosure, designed to prevent me from floating, has narrow pathways that force me to grip the mesh. But I can tell something is different. A crumb from my food block is hovering. I catch it in my mouth. I know I'll have more room to float after the spacecraft docks, but I have two days before the Dragon reaches the orbit it needs to connect with the International Space Station.

Uncurling my claws from the walkway, I scrunch into a ball and let myself go. It's not long, but I can float for a few seconds before bumping into a screen. On Earth, I might have run in a circle to express my joy. Here, there's no room for that. Instead, I float and bump and float and bump until my legs cramp. Stretching out in a corner, I wonder about the research planned for me. Scientists think studying rats will help them solve the problems humans experience when traveling for long periods in space. Wouldn't they be surprised to learn I'm on a mission to study them?

Except for the floating, the next few days remind me of the truck ride from Texas to Florida. I'm finishing a bite from my food block when a jerk makes me grab the closest square of mesh. I feel the spacecraft shudder, then hear a clunk followed by a long scraping sound, like metal on metal. Is the Dragon attaching to the space station? I hope it's a good rendezvous. The capsule walls are the only thing between the no-oxygen world of outer space and me.

CHAPTER EIGHT

SUPER RAT

I HEAR A series of clicks. *Whoomph!* The airlock is open. Licking a paw, I smooth my fur as the astronauts prepare to enter. I can tell from the flurry of voices they are excited to see me. But it seems they do not know my location. They sail past my habitat, stopping to exclaim over the fresh apples, grapes, and peppers two bins away. *Whoomph.* The breath I'm holding escapes like an open airlock. Just call me Mortimer, Invisi-Rat.

One of the astronauts floats to a container labeled "Space Debris Sensor." It's the size of a clothes dryer, but she's able to move it with just her fingertips. On

Earth, it would take at least two people to carry it! She hauls it through the docking port, past a collection of colorful flags. Counting fifteen, I realize they represent the nations who partnered to build the station. I picture one more flag showing a rat's handsome profile. A voice interrupts my thoughts.

"The rat survived!" I squint at a smooth face on a head as bald as any newborn rat.

Of course I survived. I'm a ratonaut.

Baldy pulls my habitat from its slot and slides it into a canvas bag. His voice is muffled now, and I can't pinpoint his accent. "Watch out. Live cargo coming through."

My first trip through the ISS reminds me of going through a stuffy, unlit tunnel on an amusement park ride. A few turns later, Baldy slows. The top of the bag floats open, giving me a glimpse of a rat habitat labeled "Experiment 13." It has to be my new pad in the Destiny lab. The bag closes again. Now glad to be in the dark, I dash to my ratpack under the food block. My knees tremble as the bag floats open again, but Baldy isn't looking. He's twisting a clear tube into a round slot on my home-to-be. Once snug, he reaches a hairless hand into the bag. I back up, but he isn't coming for me. Instead, his knuckly fingers attach the other end of the tube to my transport module. I realize he's letting me find my own way to the larger habitat. But will he look away?

Yes! Baldy turns to stuff the canvas bag into a drawer. Pulling my ratpack free, I dash through the tunnel and attach it beneath my new exercise wheel. He nods when he sees me in the larger cage.

"I see you found your way into the animal enclosure model, or AEM as we like to call it. Either name, it's a fancy home for a rat, if you ask me. I guess you're a smart one."

You have no idea. I look around as he removes the connecting tunnel. This habitat is a lot like the transport module, but larger, with room to float. The metal parts are painted blue and orange. Sturdy mesh lines the inside. A pressurized container holds my water. Of course, a gravity drip wouldn't work up here.

A cage cover blocks my view, but I hear Baldy clunking about. When the noises stop, I know he's gone, but it isn't truly quiet. The space station rattles and vibrates with a steady rhythm. It almost sounds like surf, except there are no gaps like the ones you'd hear between waves smashing on shore. It's noisy at the lab in Houston too, but mostly from school groups.

I won't miss kids pounding the lab windows and taunting us. "Look at those rats. They're so ugly. Who would want a rat?" Sometimes, though, a kid would say, "I'd love a rat!" I'd stand a little taller, but then the other students would go "Ewww" and drown out the smart kid.

With a shake of my head, I decide it's time to get on with my mission. I will start by mastering the art of floating in a larger space. Climbing to a central point along the mesh, I think about how the station follows the Earth's curve but never reaches the ground. The ISS and everything in it — including me — falls at five miles per second, and that free fall is why everything floats. When I let go, it will be like a drop on a roller coaster that never ends. I know this is not going to be the same as floating in the Dragon. In this big cage, I could drift away from my starting point.

Licking my lips, I decide to count backwards from twenty and let go. I get to four but think maybe I missed a number. I start again. This time I get to three, but one of my legs goes to sleep. Stopping to shake it loose, I realize I'm thirsty. I scramble over to my water. Back in position, I wonder if it's a good idea to float with water sloshing in my stomach. Maybe I should wait half an hour. As I look around for a clock, something tickles my nose. I hold my breath, but just like Halloumi, I can't stop what's about to happen. *Ratchoo!*

My eyes squeeze shut as the sneeze rocks through me, wrenching all four paws from the mesh.

Opening my eyes, I find myself in the center of the habitat. My tail instinctively wafts from side to side. I feel exposed, but then a feeling of victory rises inside. I am Mortimer, Flying Ratonaut! "Whoop!" erupts from my throat. It's like swimming but with no water to go up my nose. I swing a paw toward the sky. Well, maybe not toward the sky. I'm in the sky. I'm part of the sky, and — oh dear — I'm drifting. How am I supposed to stop?

Turning to see which wall is closest, I learn an important lesson: if you spin your head too fast in space, it will just keep going. Your body has no choice but to follow. I begin to twirl like a figure skater. Pulling my paws in makes me rotate faster. So fast, in fact, I'm getting dizzy. I spread my paws out to slow down and see I'm near the door latch. Stretching long, I manage to grab the metal and stop.

I should have known this would happen. I saw Iceberg Hands demonstrate the same thing to a school group by spinning in an office chair. She said it was all about momentum — the force a moving body has due to its weight and motion. Eyes bugging out, Iceberg Hands had spun in the chair, holding a heavy book in each hand at arm's length. When she brought the books close to her body, she spun faster because the books now traveled on a shorter circular path with the same momentum.

Hoping I haven't forgotten any other important physics lessons, I push off again. Paws outstretched, I soar across the habitat, using my tail like a rudder. It's a blast! At least, it starts that way. My snout smashes into the food block, inspiring me to come down to Earth — so to speak — and practice at slower speeds. How do astronauts make it look so easy? I push off with less force and manage to cross the habitat without cracking my skull. A little more practice and I glide without flailing. Lucky for me, no one will know I didn't start off as a natural.

Once I'm sure I can get around without bruising myself, being weightless feels like freedom. That's kind of funny since I am in a cage. Closing my eyes, I imagine I'm on a cloud — or maybe I am the cloud — a puff in the sky with a superpower. I can float, I can sail, I can soar! It feels one hundred percent glorious. For a moment, I just let myself feel. Turning on my back, I close my eyes and rest midair. My front paws float up, and I imagine conducting an orchestra. I try a gentle spin and slow roll. Each new motion begins to seem normal. I only wish Celeste were here. We'd have so much fun trying different maneuvers. After a while, I chip a bite off the food block, watch it float, and catch it in my mouth. BOTCN — bring on the camera now!

I'm nearly ready to check out the rest of the space station. First, though, I want to add a few ideas to my Grand Plan. Angling under the exercise wheel, I reach for my ratpack and find it has come loose. The camera and space pen jut out, but my journal is nowhere in sight. My mouth goes dry.

CHAPTER NINE

CLOSE CALL

I LOOK TO the floor for my missing journal before remembering I'm in space. This is the first time something I've spilled has not fallen to the floor. I let out a long breath. Microgravity is going to take some getting used to. I imagine Celeste watching. "YGUTIM — you'll get used to it, Mortie," she'd say. Using code helps me think the problem through. I decide to travel by old-fashioned paws. Grabbing the mesh, I lap the habitat. My nose twitches, and I spot the journal stuck against the bars where a fan draws my waste (unofficially known as poop and pee) out of the living area. I sniff the page. Lucky for me, nothing odorous has passed by. I reread my list of reasons rats would be suited to life on Mars. Maybe if I add to it, something will give me an idea for an experiment. I flip to a clean, white page.

Dear Journal,

Reasons rats should rule Mars:

1. Rats are less likely to experience space sickness. (Being in space can make astronauts throw up, but rats are not designed with a vomit feature. I couldn't throw up if I tried.)

2. Lab rats are easier to feed than humans. (Rats don't crave food when they're not hungry.)

3. Rats are emotionally better suited to space travel. (Humans don't like change. For example, I've noticed they want to sit in the same place for each meal. Rats are not creatures of habit and will eat anywhere.)

4. Thanks to the superior fur coats covering rats' skin, rats do not need clothes. (Humans have different outfits for every occasion. They have work clothes, play clothes, and dress-up clothes, not to mention all kinds of underwear.

And don't get me started on the shoes. They own so many. They don't seem to realize they only have two feet.)

Signing off,

Mortimer, Space Scribe

The list makes me feel organized, but I realize I can't start an experiment until I know my way around. After wedging the journal under the exercise wheel, I chew a hole beneath my food block. *Time to go, Mortie.*

Slipping out, I take my first good look at the Destiny module. The lab is like a square tunnel, half the length of a school bus. It reminds me of a rat's nest, filled with a hundred different things. Machinery and equipment cover the surfaces, and the space drones with a low electronic hum. Overhead, wires stick out through metal frames. I grab a rubber hose that reminds me of a thin octopus arm and sweep my eyes across the lab. Depending how I look at it, any surface can be a wall, floor, or ceiling. I wish rats didn't need humans to make this stuff.

I'm about to examine a panel of metal switches when a pungent odor freezes me midair. Human! Even in space, a rat can move faster than you might think.

I dive toward a tangle of wires, but the TLM — two-legged menace — gets in front of me. The hairy leg I plow into feels like a cactus.

"Wha—!" he shouts. "How did you get out?"

I try to dog-paddle toward my habitat. All four legs circle like wheels on a cart, but I stay in place. That's when I hear the voice of Boat Shoes in my head. She's telling the reporter that pushing against air isn't like pushing against water. I look for something to pivot against, but there's no time. The astronaut's freckly hand is reaching for my tail. A pellet-shaped freckle stands out on one knuckle. I push off it and angle sideways. Freckles twists to follow but turns so fast, his body begins to spin. It gives me just enough time to dive through my door. I leave it open so he'll think that's how I got out. Forcing myself to close my eyes, I float on my back and concentrate on breathing. *Haaa. Haaa. Haaa.*

A moment later, I smell the astronaut outside my habitat. I hear the latch click and feel the mesh vibrate as Freckles pulls the cover away. He hovers so long, I want to shout, but all I can do is concentrate on my breathing. I force myself to count. At forty-two, a puff of air vibrates my whiskers. Freckles pushes off. Just call me Yogi-Rat.

Opening my eyes a mere slit, I watch him pull a roll of duct tape from a compartment and turn back. I close my eyes again and listen as he weaves tape around the latch. It's hard to repress my snort. The human habit of underestimating rats always works in my favor. DTCCAR — duct tape cannot contain a rat. I expect Freckles to leave, but he goes to Experiment 12 and tapes that latch too. Does this mean I have a neighbor? Now I really want him to leave. Instead, Freckles floats to the window. Couldn't he hang out somewhere else?

Ninety minutes pass. I know because the Sun shines through the window, disappears, then reappears again. When you travel around the Earth at five miles a second, the Sun rises or sets every forty-five minutes.

I discover Freckles likes to talk to himself. I hear "unbelievable" three times, and every now and then he calls out "Wow!" or "Isn't that something!"

Since it looks like I'll be trapped for a while, I decide to draw a map of the ISS. Maybe I can use it in a video. The station is the size of a football field, and I want my viewers to understand the layout. *Otherwise they might feel lost in space — ha ha.*

Sketching always make me feel relaxed. And when I'm relaxed, ideas start to ping-pong around my head.

I'm shading the food locker latches when I realize exactly what I need to do to prove lab rats are easier to feed than humans.

CHAPTER TEN

A LITTLE VANDALISM

I WAIT AND wait for Freckles to leave so I can get to work. When he finally reaches for one of the blue hand bars spaced along the walls and slings himself out of Destiny, I put the camera on my forehead, shove the journal into my ratpack beneath the exercise wheel, and stick my nose out my secret exit. Is Freckles really gone? Or is he lurking nearby? I turn one ear. It's hard to hear anything over the murmur of fans and electronics. SSAN — space stations are noisy.

Gritting my teeth, I watch through the observation window for one more sunset. When the sky finally darkens, I squirm out. Passing Experiment 12, I slow to a hover. Would I find a fellow rat in there? It wouldn't take long to duck under the cage cover and find out. But it would take a while to explain why I need to rush off. I float past.

I can hardly believe I'm about to start phase one of my Grand Plan: make the astronauts eat like lab rats. That means one food and no condiments for an entire day. I'll use my remarkable jaws to jam the latches of all the food lockers except one. They'll be forced to eat the same thing all day because it will be too hard to open the other lockers.

Like any good scientist, I aim to predict what will happen. After all, I've been observing this species my whole life. First, they'll get frustrated. Indignant, even. Then they'll grow determined to solve the problem.

Reaching the blue bar, I push off, but the handholds are too far apart for paws. I attempt to zigzag between walls. It makes me tired. Was my training program too short? Perhaps, but I'm as determined as any astronaut. Sticking to one wall, I find a rhythm that works. Grab knob, sling forward, sail forth. The air ripples through my fur. I'm halfway through the Unity connecting node before realizing it contains one of the eating areas.

I sniff. No wonder I almost missed it. There's no hint of food — not a whiff of melted cheese, fried foods, or sticky spills. A starving rat would not find a crumb in this so-called galley. To me, it's a fake kitchen.

Almost everything astronauts eat is processed and packaged on Earth. I've watched them prepare it. Mission Control never sends anything crumbly. Floating bits would clog up the machinery. The only fresh fruits and veggies they get arrive once in a while in cargo shipments like the one that brought me. It's a super treat because the rest of the time, food up here is never fresh. There's no refrigerator, so fresh produce must be used before it spoils. And there are no counters because no real cooking takes place. Remy would not like this setup one bit.

Celeste once told me, "Before people traveled in space, scientists wondered if humans would even be able to swallow in microgravity." That seems funny now. I wonder what Celeste is doing back on Earth. Has she found any new pens?

I shake my head and tell myself, "FM." *Focus, Mortimer.*

Reaching up to tap *record*, I pan the food lockers, then close in on the labels. They show every kind of meal imaginable, from creamed spinach to potatoes with onions. One locker holds mashed prunes stuffed with nuts. This will be the food I leave alone. After zooming in on a collection of condiments, I stop recording. It's time to bend latches.

Using all four paws to hold steady, I twist the first latch with my teeth, wrenching it just enough to stop the clasp from sliding open. I continue from locker to locker, pausing when I hear new sounds. There's a whir, a creak, a mechanical sort of groan, but no human voices. Worrying about getting caught makes me hungry. I reach into the next locker and tear open two foil packets of brownies. Tossing the empty packages over my shoulder, I peer back in. A squishy bag with a straw taped to it is labeled in both English and Russian: "Apricot juice with pulp." It takes two to quench my thirst.

I throw the packages toward the other garbage, smack my lips, and get back to work. It feels good to use my teeth. Chomp, chew, bend. Making my way through the galley, I repeat the steps at least a dozen times. Finally, the prune locker is the only one left. I decide, for scientific reasons, to make sure the quality is up to standard. To be thorough, I eat three servings.

As far as I'm concerned, the astronauts will have no reason to complain about eating prunes all day. The taste is first-rate. But wait … have I botched the experiment? Could my prediction be wrong? Perhaps they'll be happy about eating such a wonderful food all day.

I turn to gather my garbage, but it isn't where I left it. My skin flushes beneath my fur, and I mutter, "EFAUH." Everything floats away up here. How long before I remember?

Angling away from the lockers, I peer under the table. Nothing. I scan around the food warmer and tall silver water canisters. Nothing. Finally, I find one of the brownie packages stuck to an air vent. I stuff it in the garbage drawer, then close my eyes, sniff the air, and focus. *Nothing*. I have licked every scent away. It's time to make my way to the other galley. I sling myself past dozens of blue and orange cargo bags bungeed to the walls. The Zvezda service module is on the opposite side of the station, but I pay attention this time. As soon as I see the food lockers, I repeat my routine. Chomp, chew, bend. Metal clanks against my teeth, and I rub my numb jaw. I have bent every latch.

I've also run out of time. I need to hide, but Unity with its prune locker is the best place to watch the action. It's also closer to my habitat if I need to make a getaway. I push off from a blue bar. The distance seems shorter now that I know my way. Sailing into Unity, I choose a coil of wire along a galley wall and adjust the camera strap on my head. I'm just in time.

The astronauts sail in for breakfast, arriving in ones and twos. I can tell Freckles and the one with the ponytail are American. They both wear the NASA meatball logo. Ponytail's long brown tresses flare out in every direction. The next to arrive, a dimple-cheeked astronaut, somersaults into the galley. When she's upright again, I see "JAXA" embroidered on her polo shirt and realize Dimples is with the Japan Aerospace Exploration Agency. A Canadian with a red maple leaf on her shorts sails in behind her. The two who arrive from the Russian side of the station are among the last to show up. Russia calls their space travelers "cosmonauts."

"Good morning!" calls out the one in navy socks. I recognize his voice.

Good morning, Baldy. I see you survived another day.

The other cosmonaut is Baldy's opposite. Short black hair spikes from his head, and his eyebrows ripple like electrocuted caterpillars. I imagine making an introduction. *Celeste, meet Caterpillar Eyes.*

The last to arrive is a man with an Italian accent

and a black moustache snaking across his upper lip. The patch on Snake Lip's sleeve says "European Space Agency."

It took a lot of cooperation for all these countries to come together to build the station. I wonder if they'll get along so well when they find out what happened to their food. I don't have to wait long to find out.

CHAPTER ELEVEN

FOOD FIGHT

A STOMACH GROWLS as the astronauts float into Unity. Baldy is the first to reach for breakfast. When the food locker doesn't open, he wraps both hands around the latch and yanks. The door doesn't budge, but Baldy does. His near-weightless body is propelled right into the lockers. *Smack!* Although he shouts in Russian, I'm sure his words are best not repeated in any language. Dimples sees it happen. She lets out a laugh like bells pealing. It stops the moment she realizes the coffee locker won't open either.

The other astronauts check latches, and each time, the reaction is the same. Moaning, agony, outrage.

Now I know I didn't botch the experiment! The emotion is so fascinating, I almost forget to shoot video. I tap *record* just as the crew realizes prunes are the only option. Such long faces! How can they not adore this sweet and sticky delight? Will they try to improve the taste with one of the ridiculous condiments they brought? It's hard to believe ketchup could make prunes taste one bit better.

"I'll check the other galley." Caterpillar Eyes pushes off. Freckles drums his fingers on the table as they wait. No one speaks. The whir of fans seems to grow louder.

Caterpillar Eyes floats back in. "It's the same in Zvezda." His eyebrows furrow in a spectacular zigzag.

I train the camera on Freckles as he hands out the foil packets. The astronauts gather around the table, jamming their toes into footholds to stop from floating away. They stick the packages to their trays with Velcro and use bungee cords to secure the trays to the table. Even an unwanted meal can't be allowed to escape.

Panning through the group, I get clips of the astronauts closest to me. Baldy is glaring at his prunes. Caterpillar Eyes looks as though he's just swallowed dirt. Ponytail is gulping water from a foil packet after each bite. She seems desperate to wash down the flavor before her taste buds can detect it. At first I wonder why Ponytail doesn't drink from a cup, but then she squeezes the packet too hard. The spilled water forms spheres, and water floats in every direction. Watching her chase the bubbles and slurp them up, I realize water won't stay in a cup. I also see why all the ISS meals are packaged in single-serving containers. Prunes in a bowl would float through the station.

I hear sniffing and stop daydreaming. Has another rat arrived? Turning, I see Snake Lip and Dimples hold prunes to their noses. I zoom in.

"It's too bad microgravity makes smells spread out before the nose can detect the scent," he says. "I'm sure this would taste better if I could smell it."

"It will take more than eau de prune to cheer me up." Dimples frowns. "I picked prunes during the tasting session, but I certainly don't want them all day. I'd like to know how the lockers got jammed. Is this meant to be a joke?"

"There's nothing funny about it," says Caterpillar Eyes. "Besides, we're going to lose weight up here. Happens to every 'naut. None of us would mess with the food supply."

"This will seem far-fetched," says Freckles, "but I found one of the rats outside his habitat last night."

"One" of the rats? I'm not completely alone up here!

"Maybe it found its way here," he continues. "Anyway, I secured the cage. It won't get out again."

How dare Freckles call me "it"! This is exactly the kind of thing my mission is going to change.

"Well, I'm afraid it's prunes and water for lunch and supper too." Ponytail pushes off. "We're scheduled to work on the space debris sensor. There's no time to fix the lockers until tomorrow morning."

More sighs, all caught on camera by *moi*. No one argues as they sling themselves after Ponytail. I realize she is the commander. I'll have to make sure to get lots of video of the big boss. People might pay more attention.

I hang out in the galley the rest of the day, sneaking video as the astronauts pop in for snacks, lunch, and supper. On one break, Maple Leaf stabs at her empty prune package with a red pen. I picture Celeste watching with me. "DWTP — don't wreck that pen," she'd say. Later, I'd spot it in her collection. I know Celeste will treat me the same when I'm back, but what about the others? Will things get back to normal?

I can't think about it too long because Baldy arrives, muttering in Russian as he reaches for a package of prunes.

I capture clips of every last one complaining about feeling "so tired" without coffee. That'll make a nice montage. I get a shot of Snake Lip yawning and Freckles pushing away an empty package just as his stomach gurgles in a rather frightening way. Of course, I don't have video of the bathroom scenes, but I can tell you they made frequent visits to the Waste and Hygiene Compartment and grumbled about that too. By the end of the day, the overall mood is, shall I say, "grumpy." Despite their low spirits, I notice the astronauts do not leave one crumb behind.

Happy with my footage, I turn off the camera, noting the battery level has dropped to ninety percent. *I hope my viewers won't think my experiment is cruelty to humans.* I'm not actually treating them any differently than they treat me. I've had pellets every meal since my teeth came in. To me, it's simply science.

I make my way back to Experiment 13, eager for a nice chomp on my food bar. Sticking close to the wall, I watch for irritable humans, ready to duck out of sight if I need to, but they must have taken themselves off to their sleep stations. I reach Destiny without any encounters. All is quiet as I float past Experiment 12. I've already decided socializing will have to wait. I want nothing more than to curl up and close my eyes before returning to the galley tomorrow. My plan is to get shots of the crew eating their favorite foods for comparison.

I squeeze into my cage, but something makes my whiskers quiver. Fur on end, I slink through the habitat.

Is that my white hair stuck to a wire? Are those my teeth marks on the food block? Did I leave the exercise wheel askew?

I know I can trust my super senses, but what I see is still a shock. A rat is in my habitat, and worse — he is reading my journal!

CHAPTER TWELVE

COSMORAT

HEAT RIPPLES THROUGH my core, and I feel my lips twist into a curl. The villainous visitor peers over the top of my journal. "You must be Mortimer. I'd sure like to hear more about the things you won't miss about Earth, especially the owls and gophers."

My reaction is physical. Hind feet kick against mesh. I fly forward, ripping the journal from his paws. "What do you think you're doing?! My journal is private!"

"Relax." He leans back to float. "I didn't read the whole thing. Words are written to be read, aren't they? Besides, it's the International Space Station. It's all about cooperation up here. Americans, Russians,

Canadians, Europeans, Asians — everyone has to share information."

The way he says, "RRRussians," I know I am dealing with a cosmorat.

"Scientific information, yes," I snap. "But this is personal. You have no right."

He pivots upright. "Let me introduce myself," he says, floating closer. "I've been looking forward to meeting you."

Edging the journal behind me, I float back a few strokes, watching his black eyes. We're the same size, but the trespasser is a hooded rat. He looks like he started out as a black-eyed white rat like me but stuck his head in gray paint. I can't believe he's acting as if he hasn't done something horrible. Does he not understand I'm mortified? Mortified Mortimer. That's me.

"I'm Boris," he says, but it sounds like *Borrr-is*. "You'll just have to forgive me for intruding. I was so excited to see something new to read — I've read everything aboard the space station twice. I'm very interested in your Grand Plan."

His voice is chirpy, and he looks at me the way a bird-watcher looks at a new species: head tilted to one side, his eyes following my every move. It's as though he's just spotted his first *Rattus norvegicus*. All he needs are a pair of binoculars and a straw hat. I begin to grind my incisors.

He watches that too, then tries again. "So, you want to move to Mars?"

He waits, patient like a birder. My tail swishes left and right. I cannot go from fury to friendly in just minutes. *Swish.* He says I'll have to forgive him, but he has not actually said he's sorry. *Swish.* As a writer, I take things literally. Apologies must be clearly stated. *Swish, swish.* The thing is, I wouldn't mind someone to talk to. After all, rats are social beings. We like to be around one another, and I am missing Celeste. Still, I can't be around rats that are OTGM — out to get me. I had enough of that with Gorgonzola. I say it out loud to make sure I don't cave in: "OTGM." Boris squints at me but doesn't ask what I'm talking about. *What am I doing?* I cover my mouth with my tail, then drop it under my chin.

Boris floats in place, one paw on the mesh to stop from drifting. I notice the gray fur narrows to a stripe down his back. It stretches to his tail, pinkish gray like mine. "What do you think? Can I be part of your Grand Plan?"

"Maybe if you hadn't snooped through my things,"

I say, knowing I sound huffy. This cosmorat needs to GMSS — give me some space. I remember where I am and feel a snicker rising. It's hard to stop. My face takes on a Gorgon grimace.

"I see," says Boris. He paddles back a rat length but doesn't stop staring at me. I glare back, and it's getting uncomfortable. Is he going to leave, or are we going to eyeball each other all day? A yawn rises up, and the effort of keeping my mouth locked makes my eyes twitch. It must look ferocious. Boris finally breaks eye contact.

"It seems I've made a grave error," he says. "Would it help if I say I'm sorry and promise not to read your journal again?"

Relief floods through me. I don't want another enemy. "It wouldn't hurt," I say. But can I believe him?

"I can't make you believe me, but I can make it up to you." It's like he's reading my mind. Boris pulls himself along the mesh to the exercise wheel. "I've been here longer. I know my way around. Maybe you'd like to come with me to watch a spacewalk up close. That ought to be useful." He jumps into the wheel and rocks.

Watch a spacewalk up close? I've already decided to avoid going anywhere near an extravehicular activity (or an EVA, as the AsCans call it). One wrong turn by the airlock and I could be drifting in outer space. Without a spacesuit to stop my blood from boiling, I'd be MNM — Mortimer No More.

Maybe I can forgive Boris for reading my journal. After all, I've done my share of spying. Can I blame him for doing the same?

"Uh, okay," I say, watching him begin to trot. "I guess that would even things out. But now I've got to sleep. I'm getting up early to finish an experiment."

"Okay," says Boris. Slinging himself out of the wheel, he makes his way toward my no-longer-a-secret exit. "I'll take off. Probably see you tomorrow night."

Should I invite the cosmorat to come with me to the galley tomorrow? The thing is, I always work alone. What if he slows me down?

About to duck out, he glances back. I decide to take a chance.

"Why don't you come with me tomorrow?" I float over to the exercise wheel and stop it from spinning. "I'll stop by and get you. Number 12, right?"

Boris's ears relax. He tries to hide it by ducking his head, but I can tell he's pleased. With a nod, he pushes through the hole and is gone. I stick my journal back in place. Finding a new hiding spot will have to wait. My next yawn feels like it will separate my jaws. I snuggle into a corner. The ISS's rattles and rumbles work like a lullaby.

When voices in the lab wake me, I jump along the mesh feeling like I have enough energy to fly. Then I remember I really can fly! *Snort.* I zoom over to my food block and, after a quick nibble, peek out. Caterpillar Eyes is attaching an electrode to Boris's head!

CHAPTER THIRTEEN

SURPRISING DISCOVERY

WHEN IT COMES to humans, rats always stick together, and I will have Boris's back. I crane my neck, trying to see what Caterpillar Eyes is doing to my new companion, but Baldy is in the way, writing on a clipboard. If only they would remove my cage cover! I creep along the mesh, angling for a better view of Boris and the wire attached to his head. I can't tell what's happening, but I don't hear any squeaking. Maybe it's not as bad as it looks.

When I hear mesh twang, followed by a click, the breath I'm holding escapes. Caterpillar Eyes puts Boris into Experiment 12 and looks at his watch. "I'll input this data into the computer. Then we can tackle the food lockers."

"I'll meet you in Zvezda," says Baldy. "The others will fix up Unity." A moment later, they're gone.

Squeezing out of my habitat, I pull the camera behind me and rap on Experiment 12. Boris appears around one side, and we float in front of each other.

"What was that all about?" I slip the camera onto my head.

"The Russians are recording how my vestibular system develops in space."

"Your vestibu-what?" I ask.

"Come inside," he says, leading me to his private entrance. "I need to eat." His habitat looks just like mine, but his escape exit is under the exercise wheel. I climb in, brushing against the wheel as I pass. *Twinggggg.*

"The vestibular system is like a sixth sense in your inner ear," he says between bites. "It tells you where you are in relation to the ground. Without it, you wouldn't know if you were up, down, or sideways."

"It sounds like a carpenter's level," I reply. Boris raises one eyebrow. "You know," I say, "a bubble in a liquid. For making things balanced." Boris raises the other eyebrow.

"Never mind," I say, climbing into the wheel to hang from a rung. "Does the test hurt? That wire electrode looked nasty."

"No, it just measures stuff happening in my brain," Boris mumbles, his mouth full of food. "I don't feel a thing."

Letting go of the rung, I drift inside the exercise wheel. "Are you sure all rats have one?"

"Look, I'll show you," he says. "Come onto the mesh."

I hop out of the wheel and hook my claws into the wire.

Boris turns to me. "Hold your paw a few inches from your eyes. Now sweep your paw back and forth a few times. Tell me what you see."

"My paw looks blurry." I shake my paw some more. "Definitely blurry, but what does that prove?"

"You'll see," Boris says. "Now put your paw a few inches from your face. Hold your paw still and shake your head back and forth. Shake it fast."

"No blur!" I blurt. The headband slips over my eyes. I push it back up. "What's going on?"

"Your paw stays in focus because your brain can tell the difference between when your paw is moving and when your head is moving. If it couldn't do this, every time you move, the room around you would get blurry. The walls would seem to lurch toward you. You wouldn't know which way is up if you wanted to go from sitting to standing."

"Very cool." I try it again, one paw on the camera. "So, without this inner ear structure, I wouldn't know whether I was still or moving."

"Right. You wouldn't know how quickly you're moving, either, or what direction you're going." Boris does a loop-de-loop. It is quite graceful, like an acrobat.

"Do humans have it too?" I ask. Maybe I can use this as another way to prove rats are superior.

"Humans have it too." Boris waves for me to follow him out of the habitat. "We have a lot in common with humans. That's why they're so fascinated with us."

I'm glad to be behind Boris so he can't see how impressed I am. Knowing him might turn out to be a good thing. I push out of the hole.

"The cosmonauts want to see how my vestibular system develops in space," says Boris, "because I was born up here. When I go to Earth, they'll measure how well I balance on land, then compare the results to how I balance and move in space."

Did I hear that right? I push ahead of him, then turn so we're face-to-face. "You've never been to Earth?"

CHAPTER FOURTEEN

SPIDERWEB?

I STARE AT Boris. His paws have never stepped on real ground. He's never sniffed fresh air or looked at the stars without a window between him and the sky. He gazes back, unblinking. Except for his bit of gray coloring, we look almost exactly the same. Soft fur, pink nose, naked tail. But my legs are sturdy from a lifetime of fighting gravity. I see now that, even with fur, Boris's legs are thin. They've never had to push against gravity. And his face is kind of puffy when you look closely. The AsCans call it puffy head/chicken legs syndrome. Celeste calls it the PHCL problem. They all get it after being up here awhile.

"Right," I murmur, "PHCL." My eyes sweep from Boris's head to his legs.

"Are you done your inspection?" Boris holds himself straight, like a butler. "Any questions?" He has a way of stretching out his *r* sound, and when he says "this" it sounds more like "dis."

"Uh," I stammer. "I was just wondering how come you speak English."

"It's the official language up here. I've heard both English and Russian since birth." Drifting toward the center of the lab, Boris grabs a wire with one paw. I grab it too but then let go. I need to move my paws around when I talk.

"I'm surprised you don't live in the Russian module."

"I did, but just before you came, the commander decided to put us in the same lab," Boris explains. "They want to keep the 'live cargo,' as they call us, together. Shall we get going?" He slings himself from the wire.

"Uh, yeah." I nod. As we make our way through Destiny, I begin to think about what this could mean. A rat born in space could really help my cause. "Do you want to hear about my plan now?" I have to raise my voice over the fans.

"You want to move to Mars, right?" Boris grabs a knob and zips past an air vent.

"Not exactly." I flail to keep up. "I want to prove rats are better suited for colonizing Mars. So humans appreciate rats more."

Boris glances back and cocks his head. "I'm treated all right up here. I don't see the problem." His outstretched paws grab a lever. It's the color of sneezeweed.

"You'll see when you get to Earth." I sniff the lever then grab it too. He knows all the best pawholds.

"So, what's it like there? Lots of gravity, right?" Boris ducks around a laptop.

"Uh, yeah." I can't believe I'm explaining this. "Basically, if you let something go, it's going to fall to the ground." I scramble after him.

"It'll stay where it lands, right? I can barely imagine it." Boris shakes his head. "And what about owls and gophers? Do they go after you all the time?" He turns to look at me, brow slightly furrowed.

"Well, uh … it's not like they're everywhere. Most lab rats stay inside. You could go your whole life without meeting an owl. And a rat can hold its own against a gopher." I release a handhold and raise my fists like a boxer.

"You mean fight?" Boris's voice gets higher.

"Well, that could happen, yeah, but usually one of you gives in. Gophers just want their space. Nobody's going to fight unless they want to eat you." I stop to rest my forelegs.

"What wants to eat a rat?" Boris floats back to me.

"Just your usual predators. Species with fangs and sharp beaks. In a city, there aren't too many except for cats and dogs. Some places have coyotes. Maybe an owl or falcon. Really, you're more likely to have problems with humans."

"Like Chester," Boris says. "That kid you lived with?"

"Yeah, him." I realize Boris knows a lot about me. But not everything. I never wrote about cheating in the maze, thank goodness.

My tail flicks. "I think Chester really wanted a dog. He tried to make me learn tricks. One day he kept shouting, 'Spin!' and making a twirling motion with his hand." I mimic the action. "Why would I do that?"

"Why would a dog do that?" asks Boris.

"I have no idea." My tail flicks. "So I chewed his hockey cards and tried to escape through the toilet, and he wondered why."

"The Russian scientists sent dogs to space before the first person." Boris shakes his head back and forth, letting his tongue loll out like a rabid beast.

"I don't think dogs are suited to space," I say. "They

slobber too much." I grab a lever to push off. "Anyway, I was not about to do stupid dog tricks. When he figured that out, he didn't like it so much. You'll see what most people are like when you get to Earth."

Boris is quiet as we sling ourselves past a workstation. I explain how I'm going to use science to build my case for sending rats to Mars. When I reach the part about the prunes, his laugh — partway between a chicken cackle and donkey bray — is loud. Suddenly, we collapse in waves of giggles. I nudge him behind some white canvas boxes strapped to the wall.

"A lot of bathroom visits, you say?" Boris clutches his sides.

"Too many to count," I reply, and that sets him off again. I try to steer him back around the boxes. "We've got to get to the galley before the astronauts."

"I'm re-re-re-ready," Boris replies. He tries covering his mouth with two paws, but donkey cackles snort through. Finally, I think of the yoga breathing trick.

"Copy what I'm doing." I puff out the words between guffaws.

"I was already breathing!" Boris protests.

"No, not that way." I close my eyes partway. "In through the nose and out through the mouth. Make a 'ha' sound when you exhale."

It doesn't work at first, but then we try not looking at each other. *Haaa. Haaa.*

"Onward!" I point my nose ahead, and, whiskers twitching, we push along. When I see we've reached the galley in Unity before any humans, I'm relieved, and my ears relax. Shaking them, I readjust the camera on my head. We hook our hind legs around a hose and wait for everyone to show up. Freckles is the first to arrive. I point his pellet-shaped freckle out to Boris.

Using a screwdriver and mallet, Freckles pries the latches, tapping until the catches release with smooth clicks. He whistles as he works, and Boris nearly makes me tumble from the hose as he purses his pink lips and pretends to whistle at the same time. I hold my breath to stop from laughing out loud.

Once done, Freckles tucks the tools away and chooses a smorgasbord of breakfast foods in foil and plastic packets. I turn the camera on and speak low, using my radio voice. "The American astronaut has chosen coffee, granola with raisins, nuts, and a packet of peaches. Four items for one meal."

The other astronauts arrive, and I whisper my names for them to Boris, using my nose to point. We look at each other when Freckles tells Snake Lip about seeing a rat loose in Destiny. Lucky for us, though, Snake Lip is not convinced.

"There's no way rats can get out of those habitats," he says, twirling his moustache.

My heart stops pounding when I hear that. I turn to video Ponytail as she reaches for a foil coffee packet. She injects hot water from a machine on the wall into the package. I think she's going to take a sip, but instead, she starts to thrash at the air as if she's just walked into a spiderweb. Is her vestibular system crashing?

CHAPTER FIFTEEN

SPACE MENU

PONYTAIL'S ARMS MOVE so fast, they appear rubbery. She shakes the coffee packet up and down and side to side, her ponytail whipping around like a lasso. Stopping as suddenly as she started, she pokes a straw into the packet and sucks the coffee out. Her face becomes serene. I tap *pause* and look at Boris. "What do you think's the matter with her?"

"What do you mean?" he asks, giving me a look like I'm the one who is strange. "She's just making coffee."

"Uh, well, it's a little different on Earth," I say. "Not so … dramatic."

We turn to watch Baldy and Caterpillar Eyes as

they float into Unity carrying a cargo bag marked in Russian letters. Baldy pulls out two cans, and Caterpillar Eyes grabs a packet labeled "*Tvorog*."

"What's *Tvorog*?" I whisper.

"A sweet Russian cottage cheese with nuts." Boris licks his lips. "It's dehydrated to make it lighter."

Baldy touches drops of water to the bottoms of the cans, which makes them stick to the table. I know what he's doing because I once watched Iceberg Hands show a class how water molecules work. First, she dropped a paper clip in water, and it sank. Then she laid the paper clip on top of the water, and it floated. She said surface tension — a force on top of the water — held it up. Molecules can push together and form something like an invisible skin, and that's what held up the clip.

When the cans don't float, I whisper into the mic, "The cosmonauts counter microgravity by using water like glue. The cosmonaut will now rehydrate his *tvorog* by injecting water into the package and doing the space bird-dance."

As I speak, Caterpillar Eyes begins to pass the package, as fast as he can, from hand to hand. Shaking it over his head, then below his waist, he spins three times. They really don't cook by the book up here!

Turning to the others, I see that no two astronauts pick the same meal. "The NASA astronauts choose from about two hundred foods and beverages, while the cosmonauts choose from one hundred foods, shipped from Russia. No matter what countries they come from, astronauts pick what to eat according to their moods. Sometimes they trade meals to satisfy their cravings." Panning the group, I record statements like "I want eggs today," "I need jam," and "This coffee is bringing me back to life."

Throughout the day, Boris and I dart behind the galley's wires and hoses. I notice they use scissors to open food packages. Rats, of course, would just use their teeth. They also seem to favor spoons over forks and knives.

"They have all that stuff," says Boris. "But everything's bite-size. As long as they don't move too quickly, the food won't fly off."

"I guess moisture in the food makes it stick to the utensil, just like water under the cans makes them stick to the table," I reply. "But spoons and scissors are still more than rats will ever need."

Slowly turning my head, I pan the group and continue my narration. "The astronauts pick different foods every time they come into the galley. Most sip coffee at least twice during the day. They laugh and joke while eating and appear relaxed. They do not leave a single crumb behind. What they do leave behind, though, is a lot of garbage. If the space station were run by ratonauts eating pellets, there would be very little garbage on this giant lab orbiting our green Earth."

When the crew sails back to work, I pull the camera off the head strap and put it into Boris's paws. I want to deliver my final thoughts on the day's work. He has no idea how to hold it steady. After a few tries, Boris balances it on the table. I tuck the head strap into a blue rail then hover in front of the lens.

"This experiment proves humans get snappy if they don't get different things to eat every day. Humans become malnourished without a variety of foods, yet lab rats can gnaw pellets or a food block every day of their lives." I bare my teeth and zoom toward the camera for dramatic effect.

"Although humans drink water, they insist on having other drinks too. And get this — some must be hot and some must be cold." I start to count on my claws. "Rats can go several days without eating. Rats drink only water. Rats stay healthy with any diet. Rats don't get grumpy. This experiment confirms my hypothesis: the food needs of lab rats are easier to meet than the food needs of humans. This fact is true both on Earth and in space."

Boris peers over the camera, but I wave a paw to keep filming.

"And now for some bonus information! On a 180-day mission, humans will need 540 meals, plus snacks. Rats will only need 180 meals. The ISS also stores extra food for emergencies, like if a cargo ship can't dock. That's another 2,190 meals for humans, or 730 for rats. Do the math and choose the right species for space!"

Boris gives me a paws-up, and I take a bow. "Was that too much?"

"No, that was good," he says, handing me the camera.

"Because I could add how rats don't need spoons. Don't you think it's odd that humans have never learned to dip their heads down to food? Instead, they create utensils to bring it up to their mouths."

"You're right. They sure do complicate things," Boris agrees. "But we should probably get back."

Nodding, I retrieve the strap and slip the camera on my head as we start back to Destiny. I can't help but hold my tail high. Boris is fun, and the experiment worked out just as I hoped. Just call me Mortimer Moviemaker.

"Thanks for the help, Boris," I say, grabbing on to Experiment 13.

Pretending to whistle like Freckles again, Boris disappears into Experiment 12. I go straight to my ratpack.

Dear Journal,

No one can argue with today's evidence! The video of Ponytail making coffee proves humans waste their time on things rats would never do. I did see one of the cosmonauts do something smart, though. It was Baldy using water to make cans stick to the table. I remember Iceberg Hands saying that in space, surface tension makes it hard for people to cry. Teardrops won't fall, and astronauts have to use their hands to clear their eyes. Hopefully my next experiment doesn't make anyone cry. I'm going to prove there is no reason to wear underwear in space.

Signing off,
Dry-Eyed Ratonaut

CHAPTER SIXTEEN

NO TO A FRIEND

A HAND REACHES inside my habitat. "Time to earn your keep, my little fur-faced friend," says Ponytail. "You're going to help us understand how spaceflight changes the human body. And that is going to help us get to Mars. You're pretty important, wouldn't you say?"

I believe I have stated my opinion on this subject, but since rats do not talk to people, I simply blink.

"Funny how our genes are similar," she says, lifting me out. "Seeing how microgravity affects you will show us what humans can expect on longer space missions."

I decide to observe her right back. According to my

sources, the naturally curved human spine straightens in space. If Ponytail stays up here long enough, she'll grow up to two inches taller.

Has she stretched yet? I bob my head, trying to estimate her length. All I can tell is that her clothes still fit. Unused to the subtleties of rat behavior, Ponytail interprets my bobbing head as a signal. She brings her other hand forward like a shield.

As if that will stop me if I really want to jump.

I chop one paw into the other, making a k*arate* sound. *Crrrunch!* It's the noise Ponytail's vertebrae will make when they come back together in Earth's gravity. I don't actually know that, but rat scientists must imagine things in order to dream up hypotheses.

My paw is stinging. I give it a lick and a shake. Ponytail raises me up to eye level. "Did you just blow me a kiss?" she asks.

I want to spin three times and feign death, but there is no room for my impersonation of Hollywood acting.

"Studying rodents in space helps people around the world, you know. It's already taught us about treating people with weak bones." A tiny reflection of me appears in her brown eyes. I curl my lips back to examine my incisors, wondering if she talks so much because she misses Earth's 7.5 billion people. The beauty of my teeth seems to startle her. Lowering me suddenly, she turns to the workstation.

I observe that a health check in space takes longer than it does on Earth, mainly because the tools can float away. Ponytail does have a few tricks, though. When she doesn't need to write, she tucks the pen in her hair. When she's not using the stethoscope, she holds it under her chin. That forces her to stop talking. I close my eyes for a moment. The ISS is never truly silent — there are always fans and pumps at work — but this is close.

After making a few notes about the strong beats of my heart, Ponytail sets me into the maze's starting compartment. I hear the click of her stopwatch as she slides the door open. There're no notches and no room to float. I trot along the mesh, knowing a cheese-flavored pellet awaits me. Whiskers twitching, I explore. Right, left, back again, left, left, right, back again, then voila … a treat tied to the mesh. There's another click and the sound of tapping on a keyboard. Next thing I know, I'm back in my habitat.

As soon as Ponytail leaves Destiny, I reach for my journal.

Dear Journal,

Could Ponytail be missing anyone on Earth? I thought I was the only one. Here's a list of things I miss about Earth, even though I have the *ratability* to fully adapt to life in space.

1. Talking code with Celeste.
2. Exploring tunnels with Halloumi.
3. Observing Iceberg Hands from a warm distance.
4. Knowing anything I drop will go down instead of drift.
5. Being surrounded by an atmosphere that contains oxygen.
6. Not having to worry about space debris.

Signing off,
Melancholy-for-just-a-moment Mortimer

I tuck away my journal, slip the camera on my head, and rap on Experiment 12. Boris pops out. He's breathing a little fast.

"Just using my exercise wheel," he says. "Give me a sec. I need some water."

I practice a twirl, bringing my forelegs closer to my body to spin faster. Boris reappears, and I stretch my forelegs out to slow down. Boris tries it too. We drift face-to-face, and I clear my throat.

"Today," I announce, "we are going to prove the human obsession with underwear is a costly waste. Are there any garbage bags up here?"

"Sure," says Boris. "Lots of cargo arrives in plastic bags. We don't even have to leave the lab." He leads me to a drawer and helps me fold two white oversize bags into squares. This experiment is going to go a lot faster with Boris along. I tuck the bags into the headband. "Do you know where they keep their clothes?"

"In their sleep stations and just outside them." Boris performs a somersault. "I can take you, but exactly how is this going to work?"

I try to somersault but only make it three-quarters of the way. "Very simple," I say, reaching for a knob. "First, we hide all their underwear."

"Even what they're wearing?"

"Except what they're wearing!" Then I see Boris's smirk. We both snort.

"The plan is to record how they act when they find out they have to live without fresh underwear. We'll give it back after a week, then record the happy reunion."

"A week!" exclaims Boris, paddling ahead. "They're going to have fits!"

"Exactly!" I sail forward, paws outstretched like Ratman from the comic books. Boris copies me, and I notice again how long he is. Has his spine stretched too?

"This experiment is going to show how humans overreact to trivial things. Did you know NASA spends from five to ten thousand dollars to ship every pound of underwear into space?"

"I don't get money," says Boris. "There isn't any up here. Is that a lot?"

"Yes! And humans are as obsessed with money as they are with underwear. They won't like going without, even for science. Maybe humans wouldn't care so much if they had tails, like the superior rat."

Reaching a set of sleep stations, we rummage through each compartment, stuffing all kinds of undergarments into a plastic bag. They seem to have every color, as well as all types of patterns — from blazing rockets to birds of prey. Boris shudders when he sees a pair of owl underwear.

By the time we're done checking outside the sleep stations, the second bag is almost full. On Earth, it would have been impossible for us to move anything this large. But Boat Shoes was right. In space, awkward, heavy objects are like feathers. We float the bags to Cygnus, the cargo vessel. It's crammed with garbage bungeed to the walls. Tying the bags to a bracket behind the other cargo, I sniff wet trash. Humans are fussy about certain smells. No chance any of them will hang out here.

"What happens to all this garbage?" I ask Boris. "Maybe we can come back and explore."

"When it's jammed full, they push it away from the station using the robotic arm. Then they fire it toward Earth. It'll burn up in the atmosphere. The spacecraft and everything inside turns to ash."

"Yikes!" I grab a bracket and push off. "Let's get out of here."

A few minutes later, we slow our approach through a connecting node. An astronaut is singing something about a rocket man. Boris points to a partition then waves his paw, telling me to get out of sight. I think he's going to follow me, but, turning back, I see his tail disappear into the cubicle. It looks a bit like a shower stall. I realize it's a hygiene compartment. What is Boris up to? Before I can even guess, he pops out carrying two more pairs of underwear. One clean, one wrinkled.

"You're crazy!" I hiss.

Boris resumes the butler pose. "Not at all," he says.

"I know how things work up here. They don't notice anything when they're washing up. You must know how people are about cleanliness. It was on your list of human obsessions."

Boris is right, but my heart still pounds. I try using code to calm down. "NEAP." Not everything's a problem. I realize I spoke aloud when Boris starts firing questions at me.

"NEAP?" says Boris. "What about the Near-Earth Asteroid Project?"

I stare at Boris. How can I explain? I can't tell him about my code with Celeste. That's not how secrets work.

Boris cocks his head at me, then a slow smile tugs at the fur on his face. "Hey, are you talking in that code you use?"

My mouth feels like it's full of mothballs. How does he know?

Boris squints at me. "I saw it in your journal. I didn't mean to bring it up, but it slipped out." He balls up the underwear and tosses it in the air. "Let me guess: NEAP — not every astronaut pouts? No, that can't be it. Not every astronaut perspires?" Boris snorts. "Wait — how about never ever annoy people?"

"Uh, no. It's 'not everything's a problem.'" I reach

out a paw to hook the underwear. "Listen, you can't tell anyone about the code."

"Who would I tell?" Boris is staring back now. It feels a bit like when we first met. "Isn't it just like you said? Not everything's a problem."

My mouth opens, then closes. I must look like a goldfish. "I don't want Celeste to think I can't keep a secret."

"But you didn't *tell* me."

My whiskers twitch. "Well, yeah, that's true." But will Celeste see it that way? Boris is examining me like a bird-watcher again.

"I promise not to tell anyone." Boris takes the underwear from me. "Now let's get rid of this."

My ears relax. I follow Boris into a gymnasium module and watch him knot the underwear around the handle of a stationary bike. Minutes later, we're back outside the hygiene compartment, hooking our hind legs around a thin hose.

Scowling, Freckles floats from the cubicle. He's trying to hold a towel around his waist, but the edges keep floating. *We must not laugh out loud.* Balling my paw into a fist, I cover my mouth. Boris is doing the same. We watch Freckles unpurse his lips just long enough to bellow, "Who took my underwear?"

Maple Leaf and Dimples float in first. "What are you talking about?" asks Maple Leaf.

"I was washing my hair and someone took my underwear. I want it back."

Glancing at each other, they start to laugh.

Ducking back into the hygiene compartment, Freckles calls out, "Look, jokes are great for a while, but this one's over. Where is it?"

Snake Lip sails in just as Freckles reappears in navy pants and a white T-shirt. I hit *record*.

"You've got to *under*stand, I have no idea." Maple Leaf grins.

"They're not *under* here," says Dimples.

"*Wear*ever could they be?" Snake Lip shrugs.

Freckles lets out a slow breath. He looks even more annoyed than he did on prune-eating day. When he whooshes off, I pause the camera. The battery is at 63 percent. I've got to remember to look for a cable.

"It's going to be hard to get enough footage," I whisper to Boris. "They won't all change their underwear at the same time."

Boris cocks his head to one side. "I guess we could take turns with the camera. Maybe wait in shifts."

My insides freeze. I remember how I used to think Chester would give me my stuff back, but I never saw it again. Of course, Boris isn't like that. He gave me back my journal right away, and he just made me an important promise. Still, my entire Grand Plan depends on this camera. No way am I letting it out of my sight.

He sticks out a paw. "I'll take the first shift."

CHAPTER SEVENTEEN

THE GREAT UNDERWEAR EXPERIMENT

ACROSS THE MODULE, Baldy lets out a shout. We crane our necks and see his head practically inside a canvas bag. I turn on the camera, hoping the mic will pick up his muffled voice.

"Where's my butt-cover?" Shoving all his clothes to one side, he sweeps them back just as fast. "It was here yesterday. Who stole my underwear?"

The other astronauts crowd into the module, dodging one another to inspect their belongings. We back further into the hoses.

I whisper into the mic, "You're watching what shall

forever be known as the Great Underwear Experiment."

Panning the module, I stop at Snake Lip. Slowly and deliberately, he takes every shirt and every pair of shorts, pants, and socks out of a net, then puts them back. A T-shirt gets away, and he reaches out to grab it, muttering all the while. Nearby, Ponytail sifts through her cubicle, a furrow creasing her brow. I lean left to fit her in my frame.

Boris nudges me and points at Maple Leaf. I angle my focus on the Canadian. Having turned all her clothes inside out, she is now setting them right. It is like watching a game of hide-and-seek that no one can win. We have not missed a pair. Everyone is coming up empty-handed.

As Boris raises his paw for a high five, the astronauts share their feelings the way only humans do. I believe the scientific word for this is griping.

"If I have to wear what I've got on another day, my skin is going to rot off." Baldy snaps his waistband.

Snake Lip shudders. "I'm itchy just thinking about it."

Caterpillar Eyes looks the most ferocious. Eyebrows jumping, he utters the rude words I heard the journalist use. In the name of science, I shall simply report he is "displeased."

Unwilling to give up, Dimples floats to her sleeping

station and combs her hands through a net. "There must be a pair here. I've just got to find fresh underwear. I won't feel human."

Ponytail takes charge. "This is unfortunate, and highly unusual, but we can't spare time to deal with it right now."

Freckles torpedoes into the center of the group. "Rodents like to hoard things. I think it's one of the rats." I try to keep the camera steady as my stomach does a cartwheel.

"Maybe we should get a cat up here," says Snake Lip. Beside me, Boris sucks in his breath.

"I'd prefer whichever *person* did this to put the items back," says Ponytail, giving Freckles a look. "Everyone needs to focus on the EVA. We've got to get the space debris sensor installed this week. Believe me, if space junk hits the station, missing underwear isn't going to be our biggest problem."

"She's the least upset," I whisper to Boris, noticing he's gone into his butler pose. "No wonder she's the commander. She's got the mind of a rat."

"That's right." Boris nods, relaxing his shoulders. "That means she won't want other animals up here." He grabs the hose with both paws and swings. "Do you still want to watch the spacewalk?"

"You bet! I've got lots of good underwear video now. We won't have to take shifts."

Boris's eyes narrow, but all he says is, "Let's go check out the Cupola while they're here. It's not usually empty."

Boris leads me to the Cupola — an observatory module I haven't seen until now. It's like a giant port-hole, its windows filling a dome-shaped area larger than a king-size bed. I imagine astronauts floating on their backs, looking into the heavens. Bright sunlight streams through six trapezoid panes around a central round window. I blink. I'd read the Sun appears brighter in space than it does from Earth's surface. In space, there's no atmosphere to absorb or scatter its light. It must be true.

"Is this where they take pictures of Earth?"

"That's right. It's also the control station for space-walks." Boris points with his tail. "The controls are here for the robotics, like the Canadarm they use for work on the outside of the station."

I peer at the controls. "The Canadarm? Sounds like a can with an arm in it."

Boris slaps his tail to his forehead. "Well, it is an arm," he says. "But it's a robotic mechanical arm. They use it to capture satellites and move equipment around. The Canadians invented it."

"Right." I nod, remembering the clunk when I arrived. "They must have used it to capture the cargo ship I arrived on."

I stretch my non-robotic forelegs forward like Ratman. Floating in, my paws reach over the workstations and to the windows. I drink in the sight of space. The view is so stupendous I have to remind myself to breathe. I am looking at the entire Earth, as a globe. The curve of our planet! The shores of entire continents go by. Mountains, farm fields, wide rivers, oceans, islands — it all lies below me. Something orange catches my eye. I realize it's an enormous forest fire. Boris points, and I follow his paw to rotating thunderclouds. Lightning bolts zap then disappear. You cover a lot of ground traveling five miles a second.

"There's sure a lot going on down there," says Boris. "I once saw a volcano erupt. I've seen hurricanes and flooding, too. Earth seems awfully dangerous. How do you avoid all that stuff?"

"It's not so bad," I reply. "There aren't any volcanoes near Houston, and I wouldn't go out in a storm."

"What if you were caught outside?" Boris asks, plucking at his fur.

"I'd just find shelter," I say. "I know my way around."

I lean toward the window. Day is turning to night, and we watch the shortest sunset I've ever seen — under ten seconds. A slender blue line marks the division between the sunlit Earth and black outer space. Seeing Earth this way makes me feel so very small. What if Gorgonzola is right and no one will ever listen to me? Can one rat really change things?

The space station's machinery rumbles around us as the stars appear, then a planet. It's Mars, the future home of ratkind. Boris follows me as I move from window to window. So much light rises from Earth's cities, and each one is its own bright spot on the globe. I think I might recognize Houston. If I were down there, the artificial light would make it hard to see all these stars. Maybe that's another reason for rats to colonize Mars. We wouldn't pollute the sky with light or waste all that energy.

As I gaze out, another light appears. A green curtain tinged with red, the aurora forms great arcs of moving light. I pull the camera off my head. "This makes a great backdrop. How about getting a clip of me talking about the Great Underwear Experiment?"

Boris sets up the shot, and I clear my throat.

"On Earth, it's common for humans to change their underwear every single day. But, since you can't wash clothes in space, astronauts wear their outfits three times then throw them out. A human spending six months on the ISS needs about one hundred and eighty pairs of underwear. Six people need one thousand and eighty pairs. Rats, on the other hand, do not need or want underwear. This could save the space program a tremendous amount of money and storage space. In addition, ratonauts have a handsome tail to cover certain private parts. Humans must cover up, and I'm glad they do, but as the Great Underwear Experiment reveals, ratonauts make a better choice for Mars exploration."

As I pause to breathe, my ears twitch. Boris hears the rustling too. "Someone's coming!"

CHAPTER EIGHTEEN

THE ALIEN

WE SHOOT INTO a loop of rubber-coated wires then edge up to Tranquility and peek in. As a ratonaut on a scientific mission, I certainly don't believe in ghosts. GAR, I tell myself. Ghosts aren't real. Yet an apparition floats toward us — white, headless, and without legs. The phantom drifts closer. My mouth goes dry. Could the station be haunted? Or is it an alien invasion? Which would be worse? I turn to ask Boris, and my heart drops into my stomach.

My friend is positioning himself for takeoff. Before I can utter a word, he shoots toward the being like a rock from a slingshot. Plowing into its chest, Boris disappears. I launch after him, striking a stubby arm and registering a crinkly sound. A gray head pops out of the being's neck. Boris is grinning. It takes me a second to go from "My friend has been absorbed by a ghost" to "He's inside a T-shirt." My heart slows to normal as I realize that someone stuffed plastic bags inside a shirt's chest and arms to make it hold its shape. The ghost must have been set free to drift through the ISS. I back away, but Boris stays inside, pulling on the cloth to wave the arms.

"Hey." I pull the camera off my head. "This will make a great video. As you know, RCHBTH — rats can hear better than humans. Can you say a few words about how your excellent rat ears can even pick up the sounds of a ghost?"

"I'm more of a behind-the-scenes kind of rat," says Boris. "Let's switch places."

Handing Boris the camera, I pop into the shirt and clear my throat as he presses *record*.

"You're listening to Mortimer the Ghost Catcher! I'm here in Tranquility, along with my pal and camera-rat Boris, also known as the Alien Annihilator. Boris led the capture of this extraterrestrial floating through the ISS."

I waggle its arms. "As you can see, it's really a harmless

prank one of the astronauts dreamed up. A seemingly silent ghost, it can sneak up on humans because their ears hear only in a limited range. However, this prank does not work on rats because we hear at ultrasonic levels. Why is this important, you ask? Because Martians will be able to sneak up and eat humans visiting Mars, but they will never, ever sneak up on a rat."

Boris makes a chopping motion, and I stop. "Great point," he says, handing me the camera. "Did you know Caterpillar Eyes is a kind of scientist that looks for alien life? He's called an astrobiologist. I heard him say extraterrestrial life will turn out to be microbes or some kind of marine life."

"No kidding. Cool, there's a job looking for something that may not exist." I put the camera back on my head. "I know astronomers have discovered thousands of exoplanets orbiting stars. Something out there must be alive." I give him a poke. "And it might just want to eat you!"

"I'd rather take my chances in space than on Earth." A grim twist seems to shape Boris's mouth, then it's gone.

Did I imagine it? Before I can decide, Boris pokes me back. I try to put him in a grapple hold, but he ducks out. Laughing, we tumble through the air. Could wrestling in microgravity become an Olympic sport?

As we make our way back to Destiny, I decide my next experiment will prove that humans are misguided about how much room they need. I mean, it's pretty obvious if you compare the size of their living quarters to mine.

"How do you think I can show that on video?" I ask Boris.

"I'll think about it," he says. "But right now, I'm going to scout out a spot to watch the spacewalk." With a wave of his paw, he's gone.

Even though we got off to a rough start, Boris has become a good friend to me. I feel like I haven't been such a good friend back. I panicked when I found out he knew about the code, and I'm pretty sure he knows I didn't want to share the camera. Just call me Mortimer, *Rattlesnake*.

Back in my habitat, I think about my Grand Plan. I wish I could make the astronauts stay in their sleep stations for a day, but that might be viewed as cruel. Humans can't handle small spaces for long periods. That's a job for rats. I pull out my journal and pen.

Dear Journal,

More reasons rats should rule Mars:

1. Shelter for rats can be smaller than shelter for humans. (Rats are content to live in small spaces, like tunnels. Humans need more space because they're larger, but they are also obsessed with having lots of room. If you gave a group of people a choice between a cottage and a castle, I'll bet every one of them would pick the castle.)

2. Rats can use their whiskers to find their way in the dark. (Humans can't use their whiskers for anything. At best, they're purely ornamental. Even that is debatable.)

3. Rats are better at learning their way around new environments. (Rats simply do not get lost. That's why humans study how rats find their way through mazes. They have no idea how to do it themselves.)

4. Rats are more self-sufficient than humans. (Put a few humans and a few rats on a desert island and see which species is better at taking care of themselves. Also, see who panics!)

Signing off,
Mortimer, Rat in a Rattletrap

In the margin, I doodle a rat holding a map on Mars. I hope Boris and Celeste will be with me if I ever get to visit the Red Planet. It would be nice to have the other rats from Houston too — well, most of them. But right now, they wouldn't want me. How am I going to repair my reputation?

When I shift the angle of the book to shade in my rat ship, a piece of paper floats out from the pages. It's my ISS diagram.

Ding! I know just what to do for my next experiment. I'll measure all the rooms in the space station and compare their size to my animal enclosure module. It won't exactly be a TV thriller, but I'll find a way to jazz it up later. To begin, I'm going to need a measuring tape and an assistant. I put the journal away, and it's a good thing. A moment later, the smell of humans tickles my nose.

An astronaut tugs at my habitat cover, and light pours in. Looking out, it feels like someone switched on a reality TV show, but right in the middle. I have no idea what is going on. Freckles is hovering in front of my habitat with a pair of scissors. He clips a small piece of ash-blond hair from behind one ear, then hands the scissors to Ponytail. Reaching behind her neck, she snips a few inches too. Are they exchanging locks as a sign of their love? I'm about to gag when they push their hair into test tubes.

"I can't wait to see what hair analysis shows us about the effects of cosmic radiation." Ponytail inserts rubber stoppers into the vials.

Freckles nods. "This could lead to new tests for measuring human health on Earth."

Snort! I cover my mouth with a paw. It isn't a love story. They would rather analyze hair than urine in a cup like those medical lab people back on Earth. I can see why. There'd be spheres of pee floating around the space station. Someone might mistake it for lemonade and drink it. I snort again, and Freckles glances at me.

"Glad to see that rat in his cage. I'll grab a fur sample, then you can run him through the maze."

For all his anti-rat chatter, Freckles' hands are gentle as he clips fur from my back. It gives me hope that humans can see rats as worthy creatures. The trick is to get everyone to think that way.

Reaching back, I run a paw along the bare patch. It reminds me of Baldy. Is he part of this experiment too? Freckles pops my fur into a vial and hands me over to Ponytail. That's where the fun ends.

CHAPTER NINETEEN

AN ALARM

PONYTAIL PLACES ME in the maze. "Ready, set, go!" Right, right, back again. I notch each turn in case Boris is going to follow me. I'm almost done when a loose wire catches the soft skin on my inner leg. A drop of blood escapes, and I let out a squeal. The blood forms a mini sphere and floats toward Freckles. He captures it between his finger and thumb and holds it up to the light for a closer look.

Ponytail examines my injury, then lowers me into the habitat. "Let's give him a break for today and go inspect the debris sensor." She watches Freckles squish my blood ball into an egg shape.

"I'd use some disinfectant if I were you," she adds, pushing off.

Talk about adding insult to injury!

Freckles soaks the blood into a tissue then floats over. He opens and closes the door a few times, cocking his ear to listen to the latch. When he pushes across Destiny, I think he's leaving, but suddenly my habitat shakes. Freckles is clanking something against the door. I raise my nose and sniff a hint of rubber.

"This will keep you where you belong," he says, wrapping a bungee cord over the door.

Where I belong is Mars.

I watch the way Freckles' arm bends and straightens. The Canadians made a robotic arm to mimic that motion. Could someone make a robotic thumb for rats?

"Now I can focus on planning for the EVA." Freckles nods and sails out. I'm alone again.

Or am I? Deciding to let a little time pass before slipping out, I reach for my pen and curl into a corner.

Dear Journal,

Humans are obsessed with preparing for the future. Here's a list of evidence to prove my point:

1. Iceberg Hands — always checking her calendar.

2. Mission Control — giving the astronauts daily to-do lists.

3. Ponytail — preparing to install the debris sensor.

4. Freckles — getting ready for his spacewalk.

5. Baldy and Caterpillar Eyes — researching vestibular systems for the Mars mission.

Other than yours truly, rats don't think too far ahead. I see now that's why Munster and the others didn't buy into my Mars Plan. Could this be something rats need to work on?

Signing off,
Mystified Mortimer

After a *rat*nap, I stretch my leg, which already feels better. Rats are stupendous healers. Also, it's easy to keep weight off a sore limb in space. I pop out of my AEM and rap on Experiment 12.

"Hellooo!" I call, but Boris doesn't answer. "Guess I'm on my own," I mutter, a little surprised how much I care.

Floating to the tool locker, I grab a metal measuring tape and hook it to a drawer. I soar across the lab, feeling like Ratman, except he would have stopped with grace. I smash into a control panel, and the tape zooms back into its chrome case. Rubbing my forehead, I try again. And again. The tape snaps three more times before I decide counting the number of ISS modules will be an easier job to tackle on my own.

I wish I had the Canadarm for a selfie stick. Instead, I stretch an arm as far as I can and take video selfies inside each module.

"One — Destiny!" My sparkling teeth fill half the screen.

"Two — Unity." I fold a paw across my chest, like a patriot.

"Three — Zarya." My voice solemn, I place a paw on a control panel.

It takes me a full sunrise and sunset to visit every module of the space station. Finally, I reach the last one. "Sixteen — Kibo."

Returning to Destiny, I stash the camera and float to my food block. Boris raps on the cage.

"Hom in," I say, my mouth so full I sound like Chester chomping marshmallows. "Cout you hold da end of a mezzuring zape for me after I eat?"

"Sure, but what for?" He twirls into the AEM.

Licking my lips, I float back from my food to explain. Boris's eyes turn squinty. "That will take forever."

"Yeah." I shrug. "But I can't think of another way to do it."

"I can," Boris says. "Follow me." We float to a bank of lockers, and he points his nose at one. "Go ahead, open it."

When the door swings wide, I see a diagram of the station taped inside the door. It shows all the measurements I need.

"Woohoo!" I'd slap Boris on the back if I were a human. I've seen AsCans do that when they're chosen for a space mission. Instead, I offer him a credit in my video.

He flicks his tail over his eyes. "I like to keep a low profile."

We examine the diagram together. It's labeled in both English and Russian. "What sound does that letter make?" I point to a backwards N.

"It makes an *ee* sound," says Boris. "It's the Russian letter for E."

I run my eyes across the Russian labels. "I think it would take me a while to learn a new language."

"I'm sure you could do it," says Boris. "With my help." He does a flip. "How about I get the camera? I'll take a shot of you next to it."

Nodding, I lean toward the diagram and examine

the solar array. I wonder how humans figured out how to convert the Sun's energy into electricity. Rats can do a lot of cool things, but I can't think of one ever inventing anything. If a piece of space junk tears through the solar panels on a Mars mission, rats won't know how to fix it. Worse, there won't be any power to make oxygen. I shudder as I remember Iceberg Hands' goodbye kiss.

Boris returns with the camera on his head, and I put on my cheery TV face. Professionals can switch moods for the camera, even with a sore leg and a fear of space debris.

"Welcome to RatTV. I'm your host, Mortimer T. Flightdeck. As a ratonaut, I live in an animal enclosure module, also called an AEM. It contains everything I need — a pressurized water bottle, a food block that never goes bad, and an exercise wheel for my health." I do a downward rat to demonstrate my fitness.

"Everything is in one small, cozy area. I do not have to travel great distances to get from one part of my shelter to another." I bring a paw to the diagram. "This chart, however, clearly shows humans need a huge amount of room to feel comfortable. They have separate places to eat, sleep, work, and exercise." I jab the diagram. "The funniest thing, though, is that they have separate spots for what is called 'going to the bathroom.' And they insist on privacy in there!"

I wave my arm for Boris to pause. "Shall I explain the whole bathroom thing?"

"Go for it!" Boris bobs his head.

"Rats have been exploring human bathrooms since they were first invented. Many a rat has traveled through pipes to reach new habitat via the toilet. It doesn't matter how much a human flushes, a rat can hold its breath for at least three minutes. If a rat wants to see your bathroom, it's going to see your bathroom."

Boris waves his paw, and I stop. "You're a little off topic," he says.

"Right, well, I'll edit it later. Let's roll again." I smooth my fur.

"A bathroom on the space station is called a Waste and Hygiene Compartment. I can't pop up in the toilet here because there are no connecting pipes." Boris waves a paw again. I remind myself, *FM — focus, Mortimer.*

"This is how it works. Suppose Freckles has to 'go.' First, he straps himself to the toilet. Then he puts his feet and thighs into special restraints. Otherwise, he'd float away. To pee, he has to line himself up with a funnel-shaped tube. Anyway, once Freckles is ready, he hits a switch. A sudden and powerful burst of air whooshes you-know-where! Airflow and suction take away the pee and send solid waste into a plastic bag. It gets compressed, so it won't take up as much room."

I snort. "You don't want to waste space in space!"

Boris waves his paw at me again. I nod, then plug my nose and continue.

"The poop is treated with a disinfectant and stored in airtight containers inside the cargo vehicle. One day, it's shipped off to burn up in Earth's atmosphere.

"Rats, of course, simply 'go.' We do not need privacy, special seating, or props. It's easy to see that humans make living in space more complicated than it needs to be. This sixteen-module space station is large enough for ten people, yet it could hold thousands of lab rats."

I nod to Boris. He stops recording then looks up with a smile in his eyes. "Do you know how they go to the bathroom on a spacewalk?"

"Don't they just wait?" I ask.

"Nope." Boris grins. "They wear a MAG."

"MAG?" I echo. "What's that? A magic anti-gas device?"

"Nope!" Boris says. "A Maximum Absorbency Garment."

"Wait." I snort. "Is that like a diaper?"

"Exactly like a diaper," Boris cackles.

"Not a good day to eat prunes!" We're both clutching our sides when an alarm sounds. High-pitched and loud, it makes me want to cover my ears and find the deepest burrow. It's too loud to ask Boris what's going on. He gestures he's going to put the camera back, and I paddle to the window. The space debris sensor isn't up yet. What if the solar panels have taken a hit? Just call me Mortimer, Rattled in a Rattle-trap. My back to the module, I don't notice Ponytail enter Destiny. But she notices me.

CHAPTER TWENTY

DRINKING PEE

PONYTAIL GRABS ME with both hands, her mouth as wide as a mason jar. I arch to look for Boris and see him dart behind a panel. *Go, buddy!*

Back in my habitat, I watch Ponytail wrap a layer of mesh around the outside of my AEM. She uses pliers to secure it tight, then pushes off. Moments later, the alarm stops. The station seems almost quiet.

Boris appears, and I give him a paws-up. "Way to get away! But what was all that racket?"

"Not sure. Maybe something broke. Could be a gas leak, though, or even fire." Boris floats closer.

"Do you think a meteor hit the station? Or space junk?" I try to sound like I'm just curious.

"Nah, the alarm would still be going if that happened," says Boris. "It would take longer to fix."

I see Boris's ears are relaxed. *I guess there's nothing to worry about.*

"Are you going to come out?" Boris floats onto his back. "I've still got the camera."

"Oh, good!" I reply, but the skin under my fur warms. The first time Boris wanted the camera, I didn't want to let go. How could I have compared him to Chester?

I show my teeth. "I've got to chew an opening first."

"It'll go faster with two." Boris grabs the wire with his two front paws and chomps.

The only sound is teeth on metal. *Zing! Zing! Zing!* After a while, though, I realize I've been bending the same piece of wire back and forth.

"So, Boris," I say. "About my Grand Plan. I'm not sure how it's going to work. Humans are going to have to get us there and take care of all that safety stuff."

"Yes, they're good at that kind of thing. But like you said, rats will be better colonizers — the main population," says Boris. "Rats will explore and make all the discoveries, name all the rocks. You can work out the details later. Step one is make them see rats belong, right?"

I stop bending the wire and straighten. Boris is right. I'm acting like a human, worrying about the future.

I realize he's asking me something. "Uh, what did you say?"

"What's the next experiment?"

"To prove humans obsess over water. They use tons for washing. Rats, on the other paw, keep clean with all-natural spit."

"Good point." Boris stops to lick a paw and smooth his whiskers. "They have spit. Why don't they use it?"

"I've always wondered!" I force a wire apart, then lean back and watch Boris. He sticks his nose under an armpit and inhales deeply. I hear his muffled voice. "Saliva works. It's like freshly generated oxygen under here."

I flick my tail. "Anyway, humans waste tons of water on Earth. They must do the same up here."

"There's not enough up here to waste." Boris angles his teeth to weaken a new wire. "They recycle every drop of liquid, including our waste."

"You mean astronauts drink our pee?" I stop.

"Yep, but they recycle it first." He lifts his head to

watch me. "And you drink their pee too — after it's filtered and treated, of course."

I climb to my water bottle and take a long sip to show how okay I am with drinking pee. After all, I swam laps in Chester's mother's toilet. Drinking recycled pee is nothing.

"Just telling you the facts," says Boris, but I can see by the way he ducks his head, he's just goofing around. A few minutes later, Boris stops to stretch.

"The water purification system is called the Sabatier." (He pronounces it *sah-bah-tee-ay*.) "It takes urine, sweat, and moisture from breathing and makes it pure. The machine even gets water back from shaving and brushing teeth."

I raise my scratched leg. "I suppose my blood will evaporate and become water too."

Boris laughs. "Maybe drinking your blood will help them think more like rats."

"All Earth's water is recycled, too. But there's no machine to do it."

"Theriously?" says Boris, his mouth full of wire.

"Seriously," I reply. "Imagine you pee on Earth. Soil and porous rock filters it. Bits of clay help purify it. Microbes in the soil break stuff down. Plants absorb the different elements and release oxygen. The oxygen binds with hydrogen and evaporates into water vapor. The vapor becomes part of the atmosphere, one day falling as rain or snow."

"I can't wait to see what Earth's like for myself." Boris snaps another square. "At least, I think I want to go. Maybe it's safer up here. At least there are no wild animals."

"Don't worry, you'll love it." *Zing!* I move to the next square. "Even though astronauts ration water, aren't they still obsessed with it?"

"You could say that. They wash before they eat, after they use the toilet, and before they go to bed. They must dream they get dirty because they wash again when they wake up. I guess that's obsessed."

"I knew it!" I do a loop-de-loop. "I'm going to stop the astronauts from showering."

"No one showers on the ISS."

"Sure they do. I read about the breathing mask they wear — you know, like a scuba mask — so they don't inhale floating water. I'll hide the mask so they can't shower."

"That was on early space stations," says Boris.

My plan is going down the drain.

"They only sponge bathe. It takes less water. Sorry,

Mortie, that idea is all washed up."

"That's it! We'll get rid of all the soap so they can't wash up. It will make them crazy." I do a flip. "Rats groom without soap, once again proving we're the best species for Mars."

I roll wire from the hole and pop out, our paws connecting in a high five. Boris hands me the camera, and I slip it on my forehead as we soar to the living quarters. The hygiene locker is crammed with squishy packets of liquid soap. We find dry shampoo and edible toothpaste, too.

"There's enough here for months!" I shake my head. "Let's jam the latch instead of hiding everything."

"Good idea," says Boris. He floats off and returns with a screwdriver. After bending the latch, he tucks the screwdriver behind a fan.

We wait. Dimples appears first. Her shirt is soaked under the arms.

"She must have been in the gym," I whisper. "Just think, that sweat is going to end up in your water bottle."

Boris wrinkles his nose. "They have to exercise two and a half hours every day," he says. "If they don't, their muscles and bones get too weak."

"What about us?" I circle the air with my tail. "We've got bones and muscles too."

"That's why I use my exercise wheel a lot," says Boris. "You won't be up here as long as me, but you should work out too."

"If it's good for them," I say, nodding, "it's usually good for us."

We watch Dimples float toward the lockers. She reaches for a door latch, and I hit *record*. When it doesn't open, she frowns, floats to another locker, and pulls out a shampoo packet. I pause the camera as she disappears into the Waste and Hygiene Compartment. Boris and I look at each other. Before I can say anything, he jams the second locker. We duck away again and wait.

Shaking her wet hair, Dimples comes out and pushes off just as Baldy arrives. He heads to the first locker. It won't open. He grunts in disapproval and tries the next one. When it sticks, Baldy heads off in the same direction as Dimples.

"Just like that, he's giving up?" I exclaim as I turn off the camera. Today is not working out according to plan.

"He doesn't have any hair to wash anyway," says Boris. "You wouldn't get great video from him."

Boris pretends to squirt shampoo on his head, then pats around as if surprised to discover there's no hair to wash. We stop laughing when a *whoosh* tells us Baldy is back. He uses the prong on a hammer to fix the locker, then checks the other latch and fixes it too. My jaw clenches, but Boris pokes me to follow Baldy to the hygiene compartment. We hover behind some wires near the open door.

Boris nods at the camera, and I click *record*. Baldy looks like he's in a snow globe. But instead of glitter, toiletries float around him. Reaching for a foil packet, he squeezes a soap bubble into the air. When he grabs it and starts to wash, droplets fly in every direction, but most of the soapy water stays on his skin. After a while, he soaks it up with a towel.

When he starts to brush his teeth, I zoom in. Suds bubble along his chin. Switching to a wide shot, I remember Iceberg Hands' lesson on surface tension. She's going to like this video.

Baldy is starting to look like Santa. He must be brushing with regular toothpaste instead of the edible kind. I know they keep both up here. "Is he going to swallow all that?" I hiss at Boris.

"Maybe, or he might spit it into a towel so it can evaporate and be used for liquid water."

Baldy turns out to be a spitter. A spitter with poor aim.

CHAPTER TWENTY-ONE

SPACE PIÑATA

JUST AS BALDY is about to shoot his spit ball, a soap packet floats in front of his eyes. He jerks to avoid it, and the wad of suds flies toward me. Toes wrapping around a wire, I struggle to hold the camera steady. The sudsy sphere is growing like an approaching asteroid. I do not want to lose the shot.

Boris slams into my shoulder. "It'll wreck the lens!"

The body check pushes me out of the way. *Splat!* Suds, bubbles, and spit stick to a chrome grill over a fan. The smell of peppermint blows out. Baldy says one of those words then, with a sigh, gathers up his toiletries and tucks everything into a net. I glance at the vibrating spit ball. A peak has formed, like the top of a lemon meringue pie.

Boris reaches out a paw to touch it. "I'm going to taste it," he whispers.

"No time!" Baldy is turning our way. I push Boris into a tangle of hoses and dive after him.

Flicking his towel, Baldy wipes the grill just as Caterpillar Eyes and Maple Leaf soar in.

Maple Leaf eyes the hygiene compartment. "That's what I need," she says. "A sponge bath. I haven't felt clean since the underwear went missing. Actually, make that since we left Earth."

"It's not so bad." Caterpillar Eyes scratches an eyebrow.

"It's disgusting," says Maple Leaf. "You might not mind smelling like a rat, but I do."

Obviously she needs to put her nose under Boris's armpit. Raising my whiskers high, I nod to Boris. He follows me to Cygnus, where the underwear is stored.

"It's not quite a week," I say to Boris, "but I think they've gone as long as they can without underthings."

Nose twitching, Boris edges around the new bags. "There's a lot more junk in here now."

I prod the closest bag but can't tell what's inside. Using my teeth, I rip peepholes and find T-shirts, pants, and socks. Boris sniffs out food packaging, spoons, and tin cans. I watch him push further in.

"Humans sure throw out a lot of stuff," I say, paddling to keep up. "Couldn't they recycle anything up here?"

Boris answers with a shout. "Evrika!" He waves me over.

I stare at him. "Does that mean you found the underwear?"

"Yes, *evrika* is Russian for *eureka*."

"And eureka means …?"

"It means I've discovered something."

Boris is using complicated words when simple ones will do. Has he been around people too long? Floating over, I see him shove the owl boxers back into the hole, then turn to chomp into the next bag. I add my teeth, and we find the rest of the underwear. After celebrating with a loop-de-loop, I keep watch as Boris steers the first bag out of the module. All is quiet as we approach the sleep stations. Without talking, we stuff underwear into nets as fast as we can. When we're done, I tie the empty bag to a latch, like a big white bow. We race back to Cygnus, and I let Boris win. Well, actually, he just wins, but I don't complain about his head start.

On our way back with the second bag, Boris's stomach gurgles so loudly I can hear it over the fans. I decide to do my human imitation. "I see you're suffering from borborygmus."

Boris straightens his back. "I'm not suffering from anything," he says. "What are you talking about?"

"That stomach rumble. It's called borborygmus. I could even say, eureka, a borborygmus!"

"I beg your pardon," Boris says. He goes into his butler pose, but his tail curls at the end. "I'm a tad hungry. Let's leave the bag and let them find it. I want to go back to Destiny." He steadies the bag while I knot the top around a blue bar by a sleeping station. It looks like an oversized white balloon.

Letting go, Boris pushes off. "See you later!"

"You're serious?" I float after him. "You'll miss the best part. Don't you want to see them find it?"

"I'll see the video," he says. "I'm starving."

Funny how I wanted to do this alone at first, and now I want company. Tucking into a net against the wall, I edit video, deleting parts that aren't usable and naming clips I can use. I've tidied almost everything when I see the battery is down to 55 percent. I'm about to turn off the camera when all six humans soar through the connecting module. I hit *record* just as Freckles spots the bag. Unknotting the top, he bares his teeth in what I believe is a grin.

"It's the underwear!" Freckles looks like he's just won a prize. The other astronauts cheer. Maple Leaf whistles a note that pushes my ears flat. Dimples finds a piece of clear tubing and whacks the bag like a piñata. The bag tears, and underwear spills in every direction. The astronauts go berserk. *Twang!* Baldy uses an elastic waistband like a slingshot. A balled-up pair of shorts zings through the module.

"Clothes for any occasion!" Caterpillar Eyes shouts, pulling a pair of boxers over his head like a hat.

Freckles hangs gray underwear on each ear. They float up like two flapping elephant ears. He puts his arm to his nose and waves it while trumpeting like an elephant. "Moowah!"

Finally, the astronauts have gathered every last floating undie. When they go to stuff the underwear in the sleep stations, they discover the other pairs we put back. Much to my surprise, they trade with each other, their voices getting louder and louder.

"This isn't mine."

"Who wears boxers with rockets on them?"

"Those are mine. Get your hands off them."

It takes them nearly half an hour to sort. Finally, Ponytail takes charge.

"I don't know who's behind this, but from this point on, everything has got to be about the spacewalk. These practical jokes have to stop."

Everyone goes silent. It's so quiet, I hold my breath. When they start talking again, I inch out of the net.

The last voice I hear is Freckles'. "The space junk is getting close. If we can't get the sensor working, we'll have to change our trajectory."

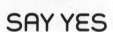

CHAPTER TWENTY-TWO

SAY YES

IT'S EASY TO sneak up on someone on the ISS. There are no ground-thwacking footsteps. When I enter Destiny, Boris is tapping on a laptop. Silent as a ghost T-shirt, I float closer. "Boo!" I poke him in the back. I expect a squeal of surprise. Instead, Boris traps me in a headlock, and I'm the one squealing. Twisting, I push my forehead into his brow only to find head-butting doesn't work in microgravity. It only makes him float away. Boris guffaws. I snort. We drift apart, but he crowds me away from the computer. I get a brief glimpse of the screen and read "World Wildlife Federation." Why is that a secret?

"Hey." I try to see around him. "Are you on the Internet?"

"Yeah, but it's super slow."

"How is there Internet up here? It's not like you can have a fiber-optic cable connecting to Earth."

"That's why it's so slow." Boris edges me away from the computer. "It links to satellites twenty-two thousand miles away. It's going to get better, though. Ponytail said they're close to testing a new satellite link that will make it high-speed."

I wish I could whistle. "Cool! So, what're you looking up?"

"Nothing much." He flips back and exits out of the screen. "Just reading."

I squint at Boris. Maybe he'll tell me later.

"In that case, can you record a couple clips for me?" I shove the camera into his paws.

Boris balances the camera on the closed laptop. "Ready when you are."

I decide to strike a new pose to keep things lively. A thin black cable snakes across a wall, and I grab it with my front paws. It will look like I'm holding up the ceiling. I clear my throat and nod to Boris.

"During the Great Underwear Experiment, ISS residents had to live without an item of clothing that they think is essential. One hundred percent expressed signs of dismay, distress, and discomfort. Even though pants and shorts hide their private parts, they showed great frustration." As I speak, my backside begins to float. I peddle my hind legs to keep in place, which makes me gently swing. Not what I planned, but it works.

"This is a huge problem." My feet sail toward the camera. "The space station is not meant to be a giant flying closet. That kind of storage doesn't exist up here. Second ..."

Boris is drawing a paw across his throat. I stop talking.

"How about adding that astronauts wear the same clothes for several days before tossing them out? What about how clothes up here don't get as dirty as they would on Earth? Also, you should say they don't sweat a lot doing everyday work since it's so easy to move things in a weightless environment."

"Why would I mention those things?" I let one paw go and swing at an angle.

"To be fair." Boris presses his lips together.

"Rats have been treated unfairly since the beginning of time. I don't think it's up to me to be fair."

Boris's tail goes as straight as a sword. "Good

reporting gives all the facts."

"What if you do some videos in Russian? Then you can say what you want." As soon as the words pop out, I'm sorry.

"No, thanks," says Boris. "I like to stay behind the scenes." He waits. I wait. Boris has an intense stare. I sigh.

If I'm not fair, people might not take me seriously. Gorgonzola will be right. No one will listen to me.

"I want my reporting to be good." I grab the wire with both paws again, and Boris taps *record*. When I add his points, his tail relaxes, and I continue.

"Humans are a species riddled with illogical habits. After throwing a pair of underwear away, it's shipped out with the other garbage, where it burns in Earth's atmosphere. Future research may show that underwear, wherever it's worn, contributes to greenhouse gases and global warming." I swing paw over paw along the wire. Boris leans back to keep me in the shot.

"As a species that does not need underwear, want underwear, or have any hang-ups relating to underwear, it's clear rats are a better choice than humans when it comes to colonizing Mars. After all, rats have a tail to hide their private parts." I let both paws go, turn, and wiggle my bum at the camera. My tail follows with an elegant flourish. Boris clicks the camera off. "A fine ending! What now?"

A yawn nearly cracks my jaw. "I'm going to take a ratnap. After that, I want to get shots of the water-making machine and the oxygen generator. Will you come with me to the Tranquility module?"

Nodding, Boris paddles back to the laptop. I climb into my habitat and get comfortable, but my eyes flutter open. What's Boris doing on that laptop? And is he right about being fair to humans? My hind foot taps. Sometimes it's easier to sort things out by writing.

Dear Journal,

I don't like to think of myself as unfair. After all, that's so human. Maybe Boris has a point. Viewers won't trust me if I leave out certain facts. They might say it's not scientific. So, here I go, for the sake of science — a list of reasons why humans should be part of the mission to Mars.

1. Humans plan for the future. Most rats don't think past their next meal.

2. People know how to design complicated machinery. Rats only know how to design nests and pile hoarded items.

3. Humans have thumbs, which makes them good

at building stuff. Rats have four toes on the front paws and five toes on the hind paws. They're ideal for climbing, but not quite as good as thumbs when it comes to holding things.

This list is longer than I thought it would be.

Signing off,
Fair and Square Mortie

I wake up feeling mighty. It's hard to believe my bones and muscles could be losing strength. Just to be safe, I hop on my exercise wheel and lope until I hear Boris rattle my mesh.

"You up? Shall we go to Tranquility now?"

Destiny seems quiet compared to Unity. Baldy is inside, running a razor across the top of his head. A hose sucks away tufts of hair, and the vacuum whines like a braking jet. Boris waves me to follow him behind a canvas strap.

"Imagine having to haul hair-cutting equipment as you explore the universe," I say with an eye roll.

For an answer, Boris waggles the camera at me then brings it to his face like a razor and runs it along his fur. I stick a paw in my mouth to silence my snort as Boris, puffing out one cheek, mimics the whining noise. He stops just as Baldy switches the machine off. Poking our heads around the canvas, we watch him stash the hair vacuum in a locker. As soon as he's gone, we float through Unity into Tranquility.

"I wonder why he chooses to be bald." I smooth my fur. "Maybe he wants to be like a newborn rat."

Boris props the camera on a metal box. "Some human habits will always be a mystery." He shrugs then gives me the nod. I lick my lips.

"Astronauts recycle space station water using this device." I tap the Sabatier with one paw. "However, recycling isn't one hundred percent efficient. Moisture is lost when the airlock is open. The carbon dioxide–removing machine causes water loss, too. Humans still need water shipped from Earth." I wave at Boris to stop recording for a moment so I can yawn. I'm still waking up.

"Shipping water into space is expensive." Boris makes a face, but I know this is what humans care about. I speed up in case he tries to stop me. "It costs about twenty thousand U.S. dollars to send just under half a U.S. gallon of water to the ISS. Six people living for six months on the ISS need almost seventy-five million dollars' worth of water!"

I'm about to stop, but then I remember a fact I've

been saving. I talk even faster. "You might know scientists have to design soaps for the ISS that don't make suds. You might *not* know they also have to make cleaning products that don't contain alcohol. If they didn't, the recycling process would turn the alcohol into vodka instead of water!"

I float close to make my face fill the screen. "Rats don't have water or alcohol problems. Say yes to rats on Mars!"

CHAPTER TWENTY-THREE

AIRLOCK

BORIS'S EYES ARE squeezed tight, and his tail pokes into one ear. I paddle from Experiment 12 to the computer and click "History." A warm flush creeps beneath my fur. Isn't this as bad as Boris reading my journal? With a glance over my shoulder, I open the folder anyway and hope I won't be caught rat-handed.

The page loads, and I scan the headings:

Animals that prey on rats: snakes, weasels, birds of prey, wildcats.

How to avoid lightning strikes.

Hurricane safety.

I bite my lip and exit the screen. My skin flushes again. How can I convince Boris that Earth is safe without telling him what I've done?

I float behind the computer and nose around for a charging cable. The first one I grab is meant for a larger device. The second fits snug. I'm about to hide the camera behind a bracket when the screen flashes that it's down to twenty-seven percent and goes dead. The hair on the back of my neck rises. Am I going to be able to record the spacewalk? I reach for another cord, and the camera powers on. But does it really work? When the battery reaches thirty-one percent, the hair on my neck flattens, and I try out my Russian — *evrika!* I leave the camera to charge, then return to the keyboard and stare at the search box. A full minute passes. I tap out "space debris." Do I really want to look this up? It's not like I can just leave. Maybe I'll wait until I'm home, with a nice protective atmosphere around me. I reach for "delete," but my paw brushes "return" instead. My head jerks back — 9.1 million hits!

I look at an image of the Hubble Space Telescope and discover it is just one of 1,200 working satellites orbiting Earth. I blink at the screen. Why does it say "working"? Are some out of order? Reading on,

I discover more than 2,800 broken satellites are out there too. And some countries use satellites for target practice! They shoot them with missiles, which creates even more debris. Humans are leaving garbage in the sky. It threatens the ISS and everyone inside.

The more I click, the more my stomach quivers. More than 165 million pieces of space junk exist. Their combined mass — 8,400 tons — equals about 1,200 African elephants. *How do they figure this stuff out?* It seems the danger occurs when space junk gets into an imaginary box-shaped zone around the station. It's about 30 miles wide, 30 miles long, and 2.5 miles deep. They call it the pizza box zone. That's colossal for a pizza but not when it comes to avoiding space debris. Paws trembling on the keyboard, I exit the screen and float to Experiment 12. Boris has slept long enough. I rattle the door.

"On my way!"

I take a moment to smooth down my fur. When Boris appears, I hover close. "What do you know about space debris?"

"Are you wondering about the new sensor?" Boris paddles backwards. I realize I'm crowding him and paddle back too.

Counting on a front paw, he lists off more numbers.

"About twenty thousand pieces are larger than a soft-ball. At least half a million are the size of a marble." He tilts his head. "And at 17,500 miles per hour, even a paint-size fleck can damage the space station."

I swallow. "Aren't you worried about it?"

"Nope. The 'nauts can move the ISS out of the way if Mission Control tells them one is coming."

"What if they can't see one coming?" I twist a piece of fur on my stomach. "What if one smashes a hole through the station?"

"You know what will happen. All the oxygen will leak out." Boris floats back, paws behind his head. "But that's why they're putting up the sensor. It's not going to be a problem."

I stare at him. *He's so calm.*

"Humans have been living in space since 2000," says Boris, twisting his tail to point out the window. "All those people at Mission Control monitor the station, right?"

"Yeah, fifty around the clock. Plus engineers and other experts are on call for emergency. I guess there's hundreds, maybe thousands if you think of your people in Star City and all the other countries involved."

My knees stop wobbling. Boris has lived up here his whole life, and he isn't worried. I guess it's true you ought to be careful about what you read on the Internet. It doesn't always tell the whole story.

I think of Boris insisting I tell all the facts in my video. I'm glad I took his advice. A yoga-style breath escapes me. Then I realize Boris is still talking.

"… I think there are a lot more dangerous things on Earth."

I want to tell him Earth is not like he thinks, but there's no time.

"Hurry and grab the camera," he says. "We need to get to the Quest Airlock before the astronauts."

I'm relieved to see the battery has reached 91 percent — almost back to the level where I started. I tuck the camera under one arm and catch up to Boris. "What's the rush?"

"Once they suit up, the door is closed and locked. They have to breathe extra oxygen before the spacewalk. It flushes the nitrogen out of their bodies. Otherwise, gas bubbles would form in their joints when they come back in. It's called decompression sickness. Very painful."

"Righto." I push off a hose as we enter Unity. "Happens to scuba divers too. They call it 'getting the bends.' It's like when a soda can is opened. The gas dissolved in the soda doesn't form bubbles until the can is opened. Once the can is opened, there's less air pressure in it, and the bubbles rise out."

"Soda?" says Boris. "Never heard of it. Can't see why you'd want bubbles in a drink." Grabbing a latch on a metal panel, he hurls himself through the node. "Sounds ridiculous."

I sling myself after him. "Have you ever been in a spacesuit? I heard the AsCans say it's like a private spacecraft."

Boris lets me catch up, and we sail alongside each other. "Yesterday was the first time," he says. "It's got a lot of layers. The temperature can go from minus two hundred degrees Fahrenheit at night to three hundred degrees Fahrenheit in the day. The suit has to protect them from micrometeoroids and space junk, too."

"Unless an elephant-size rock comes your way," I mutter, but Boris, now paddling ahead, doesn't hear me. It's just as well. I don't want him to know I've been on the computer. What if he can tell I looked at the history? Maybe there's a history of my history!

Arriving at Quest, we peek in. The airlock is roomy — about the size of one and a half parking spots. I'm surprised it's so bare. A control panel, a few large hoses, a roll of duct tape, and a couple of rectangular boxes hang on the walls.

"This is the least cluttered place I've seen up here." I turn to Boris. "It's funny they keep duct tape here."

"I heard Ponytail say astronauts on the Moon used it to hold up a fender on their buggy," says Boris. "WYOOOUT — when you're out of options, use tape."

"WYOOOUT," I repeat. "Got it."

As I look around the module, my whiskers tremble. Air movement! Boris feels it too. We dive into the leg of a spacesuit just as Freckles, Dimples, Ponytail, and Maple Leaf arrive. A fan starts up, and a soft breeze ripples through the module.

"How does the airlock work?" I whisper.

"See that door?" Boris points with his nose. "When they're ready to go outside, they pass through there and lock it behind them. It's just big enough for two 'nauts in spacesuits to stand. The air gets sucked back into the station, so the oxygen and humidity aren't blown out and wasted. Then they go through a second door into space."

Something flutters in my chest. Imagine being outside the station with only layers of material between you and space. The suits look just like the ones in the Neutral Buoyancy Lab, but now that I'm closer, I can make out more detail. Each helmet has a sunshield and headlight. A television camera sits on top, and an insulated drink bag is tucked inside.

We watch Dimples pull on a one-piece mesh under-suit over her MAG. Thin tubes run though the material.

"Water in the tubes helps keep the astronaut cool," whispers Boris.

Nodding, I watch Ponytail and Maple Leaf hold the spacesuit's legs for Dimples to step into. I realize that, as well as needing diapers, astronauts can't dress themselves. A snicker escapes. Boris looks at me, bringing a paw to his lips.

Dimples is squirming inside the suit. "A piece of metal is rubbing on my back."

Ponytail rips a strip of duct tape and uses it to hold a pad against the rough spot.

Boris taps his back with his tail and mouths, "WYOOOUT."

I crane my neck and see the suit is made of separate pieces that have to be joined. Dimples reaches her arms through the Hard Upper Torso. Freckles and Maple Leaf use metal screw rings to connect the seals between the joints. They only talk to give directions. Finally, Dimples nods to Maple Leaf. She is ready for the helmet. After setting it in place and locking the final seals, Ponytail flips a switch. The suit begins to fill with air.

When the astronauts face away, I reach out a paw and touch the back of Dimples' suit. It feels firm, like a volleyball. I pull my paw back, then turn to listen to Ponytail.

"Remember, the sensor is five feet long. Be careful it doesn't get away from you. Your EMUs are getting old, so be extra careful when you use the handholds outside the station. Space debris has roughed up the metal, and the sharp edges could pierce your EMUs."

I look at Boris and whisper, "EMUs?"

"Extravehicular Mobility Unit." He flicks his tail. "I know, big words for a spacesuit, but going outside the space station is a big deal."

"I know what they are," I hiss, "but she said EMUs, not EMU. Are two astronauts going out? They're going to find us!"

Boris begins to pluck at his fur. "You're right! Abort the suit!" Boris springs to one of the boxes and hightails it out of Quest. I want to follow, but Freckles is reaching for the pants. I flatten myself inside the leg.

CHAPTER TWENTY-FOUR

SPACEWALK

A FOOT BRUSHES me as it descends into the boot. I lean back, pressing as far as I can into the stiff material. There is just enough light to recognize Freckles' skinny chicken leg. Careful not to touch it, I tuck in close to his knee. If he keeps it slightly bent, he'll never know I'm here. Still, my paws tremble. If I'm caught, I'll be sent back to my habitat. If I'm not caught, I'll be going on a spacewalk! My heart thumps. I am not going to think about space junk. IANGTTASJ. I close my eyes. *Haaa. Haaa. Haaa.*

I can't keep them closed for long. Freckles keeps moving as the other astronauts suit him up. Each time,

I have to move too. It's like playing dodgeball in a cave. To stop from floating, I grip one of the tubes in his mesh suit, trying not to tug.

"You're ready for the upper torso," says Maple Leaf.

"Better add some padding in my back area too," says Freckles.

I hear the tape rip and scurry toward a shin. Freckles raises his arms, and everything goes dark. The astronauts' voices grow muffled, but I hear clicks as Maple Leaf connects the metal body-seal closures. The next sound is a mighty *whoosh*, and my fur blows flat as pure oxygen pressurizes the suit. Enjoying the breeze, I get as comfortable as I can and wait. I know the suit will take an hour to fill.

A crackling sound wakes me up. The voice I hear is clear. Did the astronauts remove Freckles' helmet? I can't tell who is speaking.

"The crew airlock is depressurized," says the voice. "EV1 and EV2, you have a go to exit Quest."

I straighten. It's Mission Control — the flight director in Houston!

"Copy that." Freckles begins to move forward.

My insides quiver, and my tail starts to switch. If I crane my neck, I can see inside the station, but as we move, it goes dark. Are we outside?

"My tether is clipped to the station," says Freckles. "I'm making my way to the Columbus module with the debris sensor."

It is happening! I am the first rat ever on an EVA. I stretch onto my tippy-toes. If only I could see something!

The radio crackles. "Copy that."

"My crew lock bag is hooked to the handrails at the work site," says Freckles. "I'm in position."

"I've arrived port side and am disconnecting the antenna cable," says Dimples.

"You have a go to install the space debris sensor," replies Mission Control.

"I've routed the cable to the node two end cone," says Dimples.

"I'm opening the sensor," says Freckles.

"I'm handing off the Ethernet cables," says Dimples.

The astronauts are one hundred percent focused on their task. Listening to them, I feel safe. Humans are the ones who figured out how to get to space, live in space, and work in space. If they believe this sensor will protect us from debris, big and small, I can believe it too.

I decide they probably won't notice if I peek over Freckles' shoulder. I'd like to keep the camera on, but it will be too hard to scoot around Freckles' limbs. I shove the camera under his foot. He'll never know it's there. I climb, paw over paw, pausing only when Freckles speaks again.

"I feel moisture at the back of my neck. A few droplets are floating near my face too."

"Copy that," says Mission Control. "Is it sweat? Are you working too hard?"

"It looks like sweat," says Dimples. A shadow crosses Freckles' face. She must have floated in front of his helmet. I hunker back down.

"I'm not overexerting," says Freckles. "Ugh, wait. It's not sweat or water. It tastes awful, like metal."

"Copy that. How much moisture?"

"My Snoopy cap feels soaked."

"Copy that. EV1, return to Quest. EV2, finish securing the sensor then return tools to Quest."

My spacewalk is about to end, and I haven't even seen the view. I hurry faster along the tubing. Static crackles, and I pause to listen.

"Director, the liquid's in my eyes. I can't see through it. Copy that?"

The static crackles again, then it is eerily silent. Freckles tries again.

"Mission Control, I'll follow the tether back to Quest,

but I can't tell where the handrails are. Copy that?"

Nothing.

"Mission Control, I'm not receiving," says Freckles. "The liquid may be shorting the radio. Copy that?"

I reach Freckles' chest. His voice is steady, but the heartbeat beneath my paws is speeding up. Humans are not used to finding their way in the dark with water on their faces. Rats, of course, are good at that. It comes from spending time in sewers. Nose twitching, I climb along the tube.

When I get to the helmet, I'm surprised to see how much water there is. It's much more than Baldy had in the shower. Droplets cling to the edge of Freckles' Snoopy cap, and a puddle on his forehead creeps downward. It travels along his nose and swings into his nostrils. Freckles jerks his head from side to side, but the pressurized suit is too stiff. He can't move fast enough to shake the water away. His gloved arms instinctively rise to his helmet, but they are useless to him. He can't reach in.

Liquid begins to slime over Freckles' lips. If he inhales, it will be like trying to breathe underwater at the pool. It is surface tension at its worst. He will take in the liquid and choke. Freckles' face is turning red.

CHAPTER TWENTY-FIVE

A SACRIFICE

RACING FORWARD, I sweep the water from Freckles'
nose and lips. He gasps for breath, lips forming a
giant circle. When he's still, I reach up and run my
paws across his eyelids. Spheres of water fly in every
direction. Opening his eyes, he blinks in rapid bursts,
scrunching his face as if his eyes sting.

I know the moment Freckles' vision clears. His eyebrows shoot up like rockets leaving the launch pad,
and his eyes bug out like flying saucers. A blob of
liquid lands on my nose. When I shake, it jumps to
Freckles' chin. I reach up to brush it away, and our
eyes lock. Man and rat in space.

"You little rascal," he says. "I'm so glad to see you."

He reaches for the tether to pull us toward the air-lock, but as he moves, another gush of water enters the helmet. Freckles is in trouble again. As soon as I clear his mouth, his eyes are covered. I brush that water away only to see it collect on his nose again. It is getting hard to keep up.

"I think I've got a hole in the tubing. I can feel a lot of liquid behind my right leg," says Freckles between breaths. "Copy that?"

Nothing.

Freckles can't reach the hole, but I can. I dart to the back of his leg, running my paws over the tube to feel for the crack. It is easy to find. Liquid pushes out every time Freckles moves. I think if I chew the line in half and shove the ends together, it will make a better seal. As long as we're moving, I'll know Freckles can still breathe. I grab the slippery tube with all four paws and begin to chew. The metallic taste is horrid, and my hind legs keep slipping. I grind my teeth into the plastic, certain I'm taking too long. Sure enough, Freckles stops, and I haven't even pierced the plastic yet. I zoom back to the helmet and swipe the liquid from his mouth and nostrils, then up to his eyes, cheeks, and forehead. He gives me a small smile.

Back at the cracked tube, I see the camera floating. *Evrika!* I reach for the strap. Using both front paws, I carefully pry the broken shard from the viewfinder. I grip it between my teeth, furling my lips away from its sharp edges. A giant sphere of water lands where the glass was and spreads inside the camera.

Grabbing the leaking tube, I use my hind legs to kink it, then squeeze the liquid back. I saw at the kink. Back and forth, I draw the glass across the tube, forcing myself to go slowly. It won't be good if I cut myself. Freckles will get red spheres of rat blood in his helmet.

I am nearly through when I notice we're not moving.

But if I let go of the tubing now, all the liquid will shoot out. I push on the glass as hard as I can. The tube separates! But when I try to pinch one piece of tube into the other, it doesn't work. The plastic is too stiff.

Freckles shakes his head again. There's no choice. I let go of the tubes, and as the liquid gushes, a pit opens in my stomach. Can things get any worse? I lob myself into the helmet and draw my paw across Freckles' mouth. *Swoosh.*

"There's more liquid now because I cut the leaking tube in half," I jabber as I clear Freckles' nose and eyes. "But don't worry, it's part of my plan. I'm going jam the ends together to stop the gushing." *Swoosh.* "I

tried once and it didn't work, but I'm sure I can do it."
Swoosh. My voice is quaking, and I don't know why
I'm prattling out loud. Rat talk only sounds like rodent
chatter to humans. I think my voice inspires Freckles,
though, because he tries the radio again.

"Commander," says Freckles. "There's a lot of liquid
in the suit. Copy?"

This time, a reply breaks through the static. The voice
is chirpy, and I know it very well.

"Mortie," says Boris. *Crackle crickle shh.* "When ...
—tions ..."

"Boris! The suit is leaking. Liquid keeps coating
Freckles' face!"

Crackle crickle shh. "Use!" *Crackle crickle shhshhshh.*
"—ape." *Crackle crickle shh.*

"The static keeps cutting off words," I shout. "Say
something shorter!"

The crackles stop, and the dead air sounds even
quieter than before. I've got to get back to those tubes!
I swoosh water from Freckles' nose and lips. His tongue
catches a drop of the liquid, and his face twists. I swipe
faster. *Swoosh.* Just as I bend to make my way to the
leak, my favorite chirpy voice fills the helmet.

"WYOOOUT!" *Crackle crickle shh.*

The static grows louder, but it's okay. Boris's voice is in my head. *When you're out of options, use tape.* I scramble to Freckles' back and draw my whiskers along the suit until they sense a faint ridge and vibrate. The duct tape is fused in place, but I was born with all the right tools. I use my teeth to wheedle an edge and tug with both paws. When it comes free, I tumble to the cut tubes. The tape floats behind me like a kite tail. I force the tube ends together and press the sticky side of the tape round and round. Will it hold long enough for us to get to the airlock? I hurry back to the helmet and smack my paw into the liquid covering Freckles' mouth. He draws a deep breath. And another. And another. As he gasps, I clear the rest of his face, and he opens his eyes.

"Stick with me, buddy," says Freckles. "I need you up here."

I wonder if I could get him to say that in a video. Then I remember the water spreading inside the camera. All my evidence is lost.

CHAPTER TWENTY-SIX

SOMETHING BIGGER

THE CAMERA IS in a zippered plastic bag with two servings of uncooked spaghetti. Boris watches a bubble beneath the screen separate into two smaller circles. "Are you sure about this?" he asks.

"I've seen it work." I open the bag a crack and press out the air. "Iceberg Hands dropped her phone in a sink. You should have seen the commotion. She was hooting like an owl."

Boris's eyes narrow. "Oh?"

"It's just an expression." I grimace. Boris nods, but his tail gives a slight twitch.

"Anyway, one of the labbies told Iceberg Hands

to put it in a bag of rice. A couple days later, she was texting like it never happened. The rice absorbed all the moisture."

"And you can substitute spaghetti?" Boris pokes the bag.

"I guess we'll find out."

"Maybe we should take out the dehydrated tomato and hamburger." Boris licks his lips.

I don't think it will matter, but we pick out the bigger bites and eat them, just in case.

"How did you ever get to a microphone? Were you in the Cupola?"

Boris nibbles a bit of burger before answering. "It was too busy there, so I went back to the airlock and listened to the chatter from a Snoopy cap. I heard Mission Control tell Freckles to return, but then the sound went out. I kept listening, and after forever I heard you through the static," Boris exclaims. "I didn't know what you were doing until you started talking to Freckles."

"You saved us, Boris." I float as still as I can so he'll see I'm serious. "Thank you."

"You did the saving." Boris ducks his head. "I just helped a little."

"You did more than that," I say, but I can tell Boris

would rather not talk about it. He doesn't want even fifteen minutes of fame.

When we're done chomping on tomato and hamburger, I put the camera back in my habitat.

"I still can't believe you went on a spacewalk!" Boris says when I pop back out. "What was it like?"

I take a deep breath. How can I explain? Floating to the window in Destiny, I look out. Boris floats beside me, and we watch the Moon rise.

"I could only see for a little while — when I was in the helmet — but floating out there with nothing but a spacesuit between me and Earth, it was ... well, something." I can't seem to find the words to explain how it made me tremble and feel so very small. But it was because I was small that I could help Freckles. His hands, stuck in the spacesuit gloves, couldn't reach inside the helmet. If I hadn't been there to brush the water off his mouth and nose, he would have drowned. And if I hadn't been there to clear his eyes, he wouldn't have found his way back to the airlock. We'd both still be out there. I shudder.

Before the spacewalk, I didn't think about why the surface tension of water was such a big deal. But it forced Freckles to stop again and again as he pulled us back to the ISS. Each time, after swishing the water away, I fit myself inside the warm curve of his neck and stared out the helmet. When I looked at Earth, green and blue and brown, my whiskers quivered. The thin blue line that separated night and day in space made something build inside my chest. Like I had a new responsibility. Not to make sure rats got to Mars, but something bigger.

I didn't know what it meant, and I couldn't explain it to Boris. At least not yet. It was something I had to think about, maybe write about in my journal. I know rats will never get to Mars without humans, but now Freckles knows rats do belong in space, and that seems like enough. I somehow showed it best when I wasn't even trying. When I wasn't thinking about my Grand Plan or comparing rats and humans. I no longer feel like I have to prove something to Gorgonzola or people like Chester. No one can take away those moments in space, rat and man side by side and glad of it — knowing we could work together and achieve even more.

Boris cocks his head, waiting for me to finish. Paws at my sides, all I can do is shrug.

"I bet you can find another camera back on Earth." Boris turns from the window. "Maybe use trick photography to redo parts of the experiments."

"Maybe," I say, turning to face him. Boris has helped me so many times. He's more than a good friend — this cosmorat is a lifesaver. He'll understand when I find the right words to explain what I'm thinking — that maybe it doesn't matter if my videos are lost forever. I float over and give him a friendly shove. He pretends to fall back, then flips and comes at me from above. We tussle in the air, butting heads as best we can in microgravity, then push back from each other to rest.

Our time on the space station is nearly over. We're scheduled to return to Earth on the Russian spacecraft called Soyuz. I'll get to see Russia's Star City, then Boris will travel with me to Houston. I'm looking forward to showing him around the planet. But first, I have something to show him up here.

"Hey," I say. "Come to the computer for a sec." Boris floats over and watches me open a browser. I type: *how rats outsmart predators.*

I feel him straighten.

"Look." I nod at the screen. "Sixty thousand and three hundred hits. Check out the subject headings."

Rats, smartest animal on the planet.

Most predators can't outsmart rats.

Rats use their highly developed senses to outwit enemies.

"How did you know?" Boris asks. His tail is moving into its sword position. My stomach twists, but I decide to come clean. Friends have to be honest with each other.

"I looked at your Internet history," I say. Boris gives me the same stare I gave him when I caught him with my journal. My hind foot starts to tap.

"I'm sorry. I shouldn't have done it." I start to talk fast in case he's about to blow his top. "I just want you to know it's not that dangerous. You only have to take normal safety precautions, just like in space. Look before you leap kind of stuff. The owl wouldn't have been able to grab me if I'd been paying attention. And the gopher was just unfriendly, not dangerous. Another thing, I've never heard of a rat getting struck by lightning, and anyway, you won't be alone. I'll be watching out for you …"

My voice trails off.

Boris blinks. "If I'd told you when you saw me on the computer," he says, "I wouldn't have been worrying for so long. I didn't want you to think I was a scaredy-rat."

"I'd never think that! I was worrying too — about meteors. You convinced me that we're safe. You're not mad I snooped?"

"Only a little." Boris floats close and shoves his

184 • JOAN MARIE GALAT

shoulder into mine. I somersault and push him back with my hind feet. We wrestle a bit, then Boris floats back. "I guess there's some truth to the saying 'curiosity killed the rat.'"

Before I can reply, we hear voices and dive into our AEMs. Ponytail and Baldy arrive with two transporter modules and leave us alone to find our way in. I grab the baggie with the camera, along with my journal and pen, and haul everything across. This transport module is much smaller. I can barely turn around and have to shove everything under my butt. Next thing we know, our habitats are clicked into the Soyuz Descent Module. We're not alone. Freckles, Dimples, and Caterpillar Eyes are strapped into seats, specially molded to fit their bodies. They barely have an inch to move either.

Caterpillar Eyes is the Soyuz commander. He un-docks the Soyuz from the ISS, and we circle the Earth. After three hours, Caterpillar Eyes rotates the con-troller, and eight thrusters fire. We head for the entry point four hundred thousand feet above the Earth.

Boris and I peek from our modules. I've never been to Russia, and he's never been to Earth. I wonder if his stomach is fluttering like mine.

Eight minutes later, the Soyuz enters Earth's atmosphere. A roar fills my ears, and I'm pushed to the top of my module. It's hard to breathe, and I can't move. The scientist in me notes that I'd be tossed about if I were in a bigger space. The everyday rat part of me can't think about it. I want to know what's happening. *Is this a normal landing? Are we crashing? Is Boris okay?* I can't understand the Russian words going back and forth between Caterpillar Eyes and Star City, but eight minutes later, parachutes slow us from 755 feet per second to five feet per second, then even slower. The Soyuz bounces across a plain in Kazakhstan.

CHAPTER TWENTY-SEVEN

FACING THE PAST

THE LAB RATS cheer when Boris and I arrive in Houston. What's going on? Celeste explains as soon as we're alone.

"Everyone listened to the live feed of the spacewalk," she says. "Afterwards, Gorgonzola zinged his cage bars to make everyone pay attention. Then he gave a speech!"

"A speech!" I echo. My ears don't know whether to rise or lay flat.

"Gorgonzola admitted he was the one to put sneezeweed in Halloumi's cage." Celeste leans so close I can smell her pellet breath. "He told them you only changed the notches to stop him from cheating his way to space."

I scratch behind an ear. It seems Gorgonzola did something awfully tough — maybe even tougher than coming back from a spacewalk. Gorgonzola admitted he was wrong.

"He even said he was proud of you!" Celeste looks as happy as if she found a new pen.

I feel my ears relax, but the rest of the day, my mind returns to Celeste's words. Did Gorgonzola really mean it? I get my answer after the lights dim and the last human leaves. Gorgonzola pads across the counter. My stomach flutters as he reaches my cage. He looks me in the eyes. "I'm sorry, Mortimer."

Gorgonzola disappears into the cabinetry before I can reply. A slow smile reaches my lips. I stick my head into my aspen chips and inhale their fresh, woody scent. It feels good to be home.

The lab is dark when the patter of pawsteps wake me. I watch through half-closed eyes as Halloumi dribbles a hill of corn kernels into my cage. He waggles his ears when I stand up. I waggle mine back. When he's gone, I take an armload of kernels and trickle them through Gorgonzola's bars. Now it's like nothing ever happened, but better. Everyone likes Gorgonzola more now. Especially me.

Two months later, Iceberg Hands pushes the whiteboard up to the maze. It reminds me of the race that got me to space, but things are different around here now. I watch Iceberg Hands grab a black marker and scrawl the names of all the lab rats being tested: Halloumi, Romano, Feta, Celeste, Munster, Gorgonzola, Mortimer, and Boris.

"Why aren't Tillamook and Wigmore racing?" I ask Celeste.

"They got picked for a mission while you were gone," she says. "This test is for a different blastoff."

Beside me, Boris sighs and flicks his tail. "Do you think I have a chance? I feel so slow and heavy on Earth."

"I'm sure you have a chance," I reply, but it's awkward. We both want to go back to space, but for Boris, it's home.

"Just remember the notching system," says Celeste. She's talking to Boris but looking at me. "A slash through the notch means don't go that way."

Boris nods. "Got it."

"Iceberg Hands wouldn't have put you on the list

if she didn't think you could do it," says Celeste. "A
month ago, you didn't have the energy."

She's right. After we were picked up in Kazakhstan
and taken to Star City, my legs were weak from not
using them as much as I had on Earth. Boris had an
even harder time. His muscles had to get used to working in gravity for the first time. I guess we both should
have used our exercise wheels more. At first, all we
cared about was sleep. But then we found ourselves
on a jet to Houston, and Iceberg Hands had other
ideas. She kept putting us in our exercise wheels. Her
chilly fingers made us want to run to warm up.

Now we're both as fit as the other rats, but Boris still
forgets he's not in space. I see him let go of things in
the air. When they fall instead of floating, he shakes
his head and mutters in Russian. Once he leaped from
his exercise wheel and slammed into his wood chips.
I know he expected to sail across his cage. We laughed,
but I saw his tail flick. I know he's homesick.

Celeste tries to cheer him up. "You'll get back to
space one day."

"YGBTSOD," I add. Celeste raises her eyebrows at
me.

"Boris knows," I say. I didn't think it was possible,

but her eyebrows go even higher. I can't fink on Boris reading my journal, but I need to be honest with Celeste. How do I fix this? I'm taking too long to say something. Then I realize Celeste heard Boris use code during the spacewalk. She knew all along. Celeste gives me a rat hug — a tail around the shoulder — and I know it's okay.

Across the lab, Iceberg Hands picks up her stethoscope. "Okay," she calls, "time for health checks."

Boris and I warm up with a few quick yoga stretches. Iceberg Hands inspects everyone, then pulls out her stopwatch. Halloumi is first. Without a scent trail to follow, his time is higher than usual: 131 seconds. We watch Romano, then Feta, trot through the maze and mark the path as they go. I know they both still want to stay on Earth. Iceberg Hands records their times then puts Celeste at the starting gate. She goes fast enough to get a good score, but not fast enough to get chosen.

Munster is next. He zips through the maze in just 120 seconds. It's the best time so far, but Gorgonzola is next. We watch Iceberg Hands lift the gate. Gorgonzola dashes forward, sniffing, turning, doubling back. He finishes at 118 and smirks at Munster, who rocks on his paws.

I'm next. My stomach curdles as Iceberg Hands resets the stopwatch. I so want to float again. And what if I could go on another spacewalk?

Iceberg Hands shouts, "Go!" I dash forward, sniffing and watching for notches. The marks on the walls are not very clear. There's so many from all the different times the maze has been used. I can't stop myself. I start to change the notches. When I reach the end, I'm out of breath.

"118 seconds," Iceberg Hands calls out. I'm tied with Gorgonzola. I keep my eyes down on the way out of the maze.

Iceberg Hands resets the stopwatch and picks up Boris. I turn to watch. Right, right, left. He zips through the maze. I'm holding my breath when Iceberg Hands picks up the marker and writes 110 seconds.

"You're going back to space, buddy," she says, circling Boris's name. "Enjoy your last few weeks on Earth."

I cheer, and everyone looks at me like I'm crazy. Except Celeste and Boris. Their ears have dropped, and both are grinning.

Later, when the humans have left, Boris tells everyone how he made it through so fast.

"At first I was confused. There were just too many notches. I'm not used to the system. But then I saw the

Russian letter for E. I knew Mortimer was making it easier for me."

I feel my skin heat up under my fur. "You'd do the same for me," is all I can come up with.

On Boris's last night, we stay up late playing catch.

"I wish we knew how long your mission will be," I say, lobbing the pellet to Boris.

"All I know is NASA wants me back in Houston," says Boris, turning the pellet over in his paws. "They're taking over the experiment to see how my vestibular system reacts to going between Earth and space." He tosses the pellet to Celeste.

Catching it in her mouth, she swallows. "Oops, sorry!"

"Do you think you'll ever change your mind about going to space?" Boris asks.

"I might, if we can all go to Mars together," she says. "I like a little gravity."

"It's only a matter of time," says Boris.

I nod. Even though I still dream of seeing rats on Mars, I know NASA needs years to invent the technology it will take to get there. I also know Freckles won't forget our time together. He visits me in the lab sometimes, and one day, a camera crew came too. Freckles told everyone what happened on the spacewalk, and they showed the clip on the news. Now when tours come through, Iceberg Hands points me out as Mortimer, Lifesaving Rat. I want to be fair and tell them Boris helped too, but he wouldn't like that. Anyway, it's not possible. Humans don't speak Rat.

I haven't forgotten that Freckles saved me too. He's the one who got us back inside the ISS. I still want rats to colonize Mars, but I want humans alongside us, not just to make the rockets and spacecraft, but so we can watch out for one another. Just like all the countries that worked together to build the space station in the first place.

Celeste notices me daydreaming. She cocks her head, and Boris turns to look. "You're planning something, aren't you, Mortie?"

I turn a chip over in my paws, hoping I look casual. "Well, I do have an idea for a sort of ground-based mission while we wait for Boris to come back."

They wait.

"Don't you think lab rats should have rights?" Dropping the chip, I jump to all fours. "Wouldn't it be nice to not feel like we're standing on a glacier every time Iceberg Hands picks us up? If we can put people in space, surely we can find a way to warm the hands of a labbie."

"Romano's got that glove." Celeste reaches for another pellet. "There must be more."

"Yes!" I nod. "That can go on my list. By the time you're back, Boris, this problem is going to be solved, or my name's not —"

"Mortimer the Melter?" Boris blows hot breath on his paws. "Thermo-Rat?"

Zinging the pellet to Boris, Celeste turns to me. "Mortie, are you going to do it in a diplomatic way or take a more ratty approach?"

"Oh, sure, I'll be diplomatic. Isn't that my style?" I turn so Celeste can't see my face.

Boris laughs that donkey bray of his and lobs the pellet at my head. Sailing high, it zings along the cage bars.

Next door, Gorgonzola mutters about the noise.

Ignoring him, I try to look sincere. The angle of Celeste's whiskers tells me I'm not succeeding. Tail waving like a flag, I say it anyway. "Just call me Mortimer, Diplo-Rat."

ACKNOWLEDGEMENTS

This book began as an idea for a nonfiction title that featured a journal-keeping lab rat on the International Space Station. I wanted to share the awe I feel knowing astronauts live and work in space on a continuous basis. Perhaps I could have chosen a more popular species for my characters, but I wanted to be as factual as possible within the story. *Rattus norvegicus* have lived on the ISS, and I hope you found their unique abilities added to the adventure.

My research included an invaluable trip to NASA's

Space Center Houston. The Space Exploration Educators Conference I attended provided a behind-the-scenes look at space missions and the technologies being developed to explore the universe. I came away more inspired than ever.

As my manuscript evolved, readers seemed to appreciate Mortimer's charm. More than one suggested moving him from sidebar entries to a character in a novel. After deciding to explore this approach, I was honored to be recognized with the Martha Weston Grant. This award supports the efforts of one worldwide member of the Society of Children's Book Writers and Illustrators (SCBWI) changing genres, and funds attendance at the SCBWI conference in Los Angeles. I used the opportunity to build on my fiction writing skills and have my work critiqued.

The space industry is constantly evolving, and I was determined to have my story reflect real science. I traveled to NASA's Kennedy Space Centre in Cape Canaveral, Florida to collect the most up-to-date exploration information. I watched a nighttime SpaceX Falcon Heavy lift off, attended astronaut-led tours, and asked a myriad of questions.

I'm pleased to acknowledge the Alberta Foundation of the Arts for supporting the research and writing of this manuscript. Thanks to the Hairston family, who established the Martha Weston Grant, and the SCBWI who also supported my attendance in L.A.

I offer my gratitude to Stacey Kondla, The Rights Factory, for finding this book the perfect home. Thanks to DCB publisher Barry Jowett for his enthusiasm and thoughtful story input, editor Andrea Waters for her expert attention to detail, and the entire DCB team for supporting my efforts and helping bring this book to readers.

Thanks to Daniel Nayeri for taking the time to talk and send me an advance reader copy of a middle grade title that provided a current example of how to best write talking animals. My appreciation extends to editor Bev Katz Rosenbaum who helped me fine tune the manuscript before submission. Her insights helped me grow in the most satisfying way. Warm thanks to Karen Grencik at Red Fox Literary, who believed in my work at first read, and helped me connect with industry professionals throughout our working relationship. Thanks to Claire J. Scavuzzo, Ph.D., for answering questions about lab rats and Vickie Kloeris, MS, CFS, former Manager International Space Station Food System at NASA's Johnson Space Center for sharing the intricacies of space food. With regret for any omissions made here, I offer earnest gratitude to all that aided my process.

Special literary hugs go to the friends who listened to me talk about Mortimer and provided insights that helped me along the way: Jacqueline Guest, Karen Spafford-Fitz, Lorna Schultz-Nicholson, Debby Waldman, Rita Feutl, Maggie Field, and Leanne Myggland-Carter. Thanks also to my husband Grant Wiens, along with my family, whose love and support helped see this story travel from keyboard to book.

Joan Marie Galat is an award-winning author of more than twenty books for children and adults, with translations in eight languages. She is best known for her science books for children, especially her astronomy titles, and her interest in everything outer space. Her books have won and been nominated for numerous awards including the Crystal Kite, Skipping Stones, Rocky Mountain, Red Cedar, Hackmatack, Moonbeam, and Green Prize for Sustainable Literature, among others. She is the 2018 recipient of the Martha Weston Grant, awarded annually to one worldwide member of the Society of Children's Book Writers and Illustrators. Galat lives in Alberta, near Edmonton. Visit www.joangalat.com to arrange literacy-building science and engineering presentations at your school.